FRANKENWEENIE

A Graphic Novel

Adapted by Alessandro Ferrari
Illustrated by Helen Chen and Jorgen Klubien
Art direction by Rick Heinrichs

Executive Producer: Don Hahn
Based on a screenplay by Lenny Ripps
Based on an original idea by Tim Burton
Screenplay by John August
Produced by Tim Burton and Allison Abbate
Directed by Tim Burton

DISNEP PRESS
New York • Los Angeles

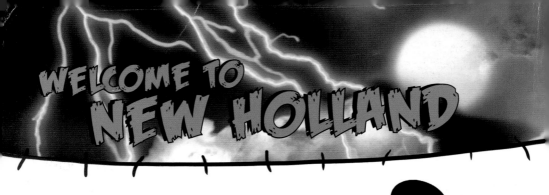

WELCOME TO NEW HOLLAND

VICTOR FRANKENSTEIN

"I just wanted my dog back."

Victor Frankenstein does not go out with other kids very much. He's got all he needs in his **makeshift laboratory**: he shoots homemade movies and conducts science experiments. Victor would do **anything out of love for his dog**. When Sparky dies in a car accident, Victor uses his scientific ingenuity to **bring him back to life**.

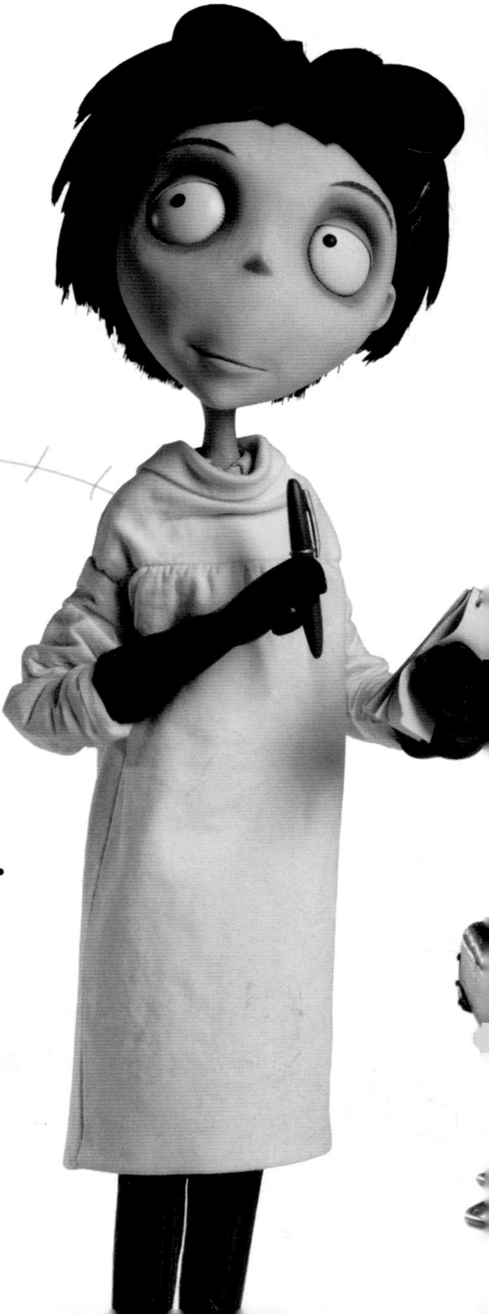

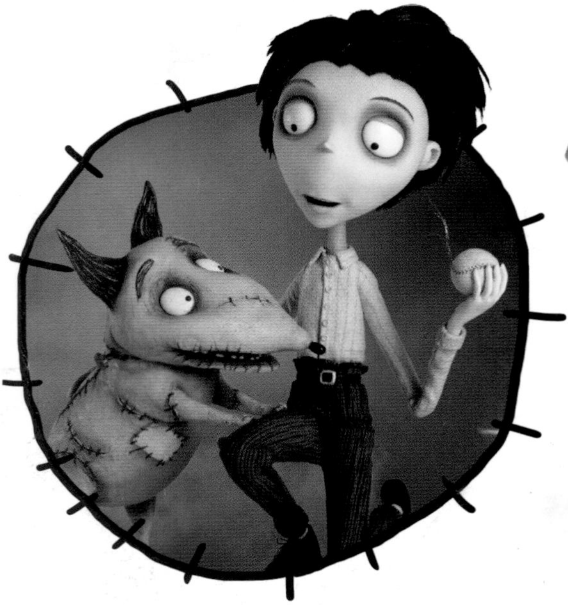

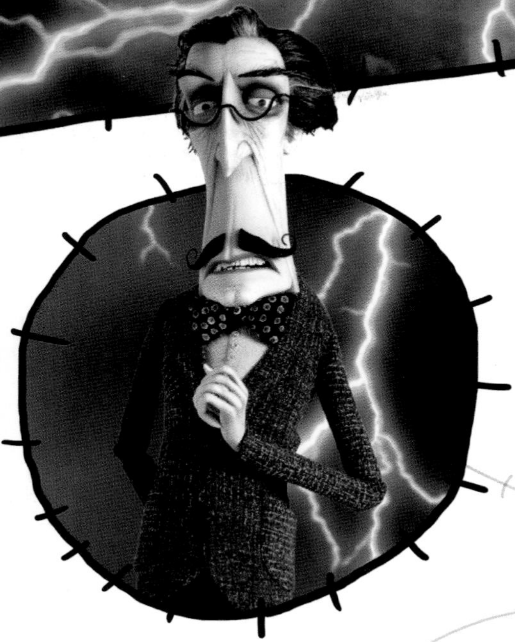

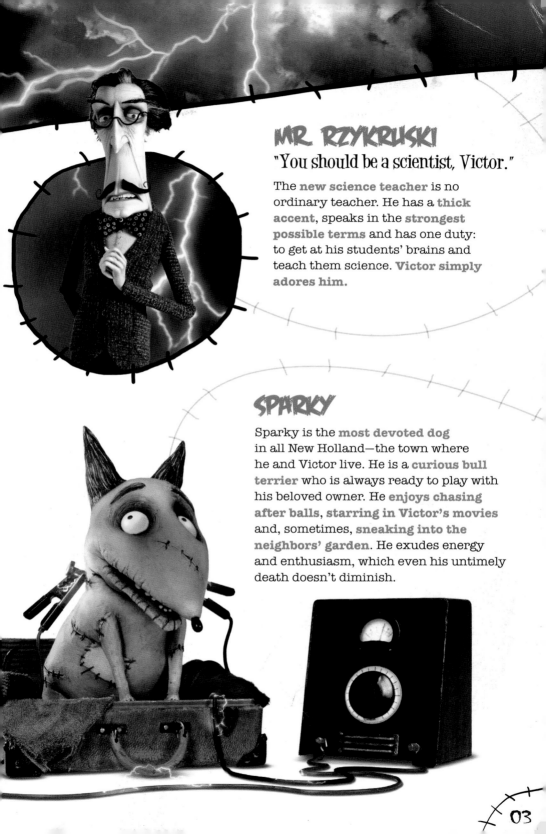

MR. RZYKRUSKI

"You should be a scientist, Victor."

The **new science teacher** is no ordinary teacher. He has a **thick accent**, speaks in the **strongest possible terms** and has one duty: to get at his students' brains and teach them science. **Victor simply adores him.**

SPARKY

Sparky is the **most devoted dog** in all New Holland—the town where he and Victor live. He is a **curious bull terrier** who is always ready to play with his beloved owner. He **enjoys chasing after balls, starring in Victor's movies** and, sometimes, **sneaking into the neighbors' garden**. He exudes energy and enthusiasm, which even his untimely death doesn't diminish.

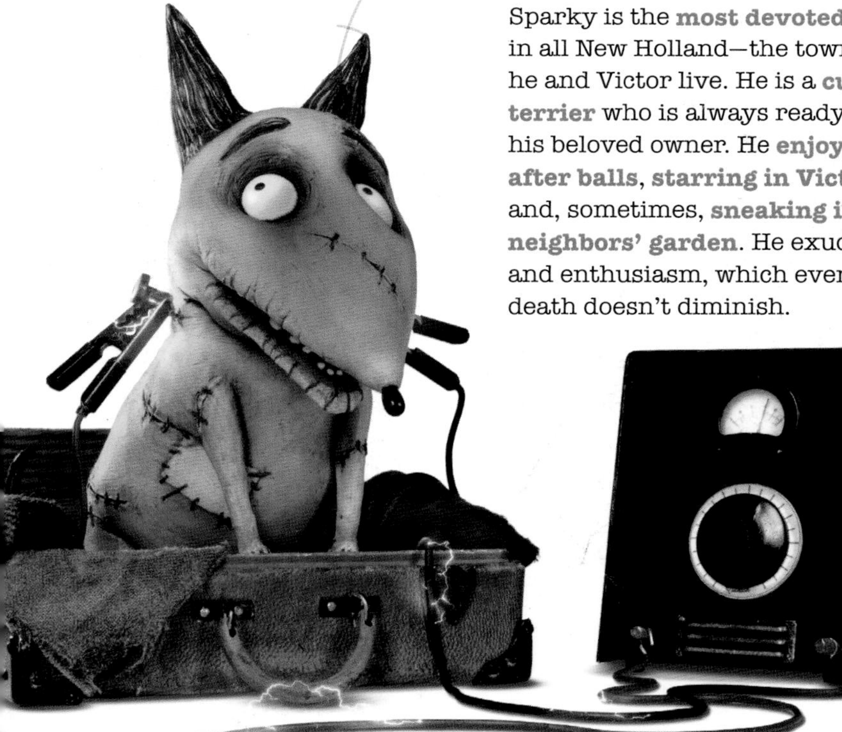

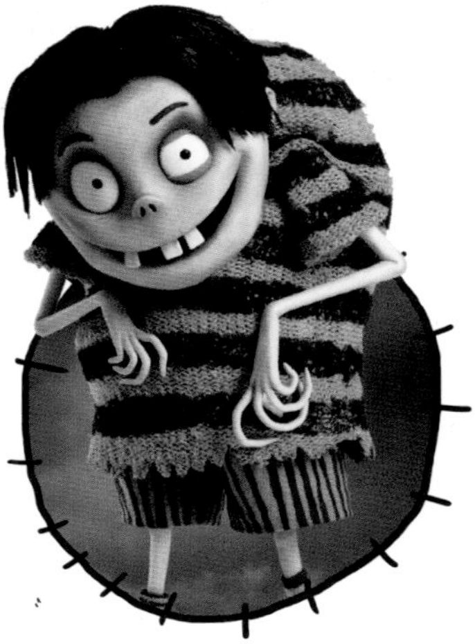

EDGAR

"I think I know what you know I know."

Edgar "E" Gore just **wants to be Victor's partner** for the **science fair**. When he discovers Victor's secret about Sparky he gets what he wants. Unfortunately, he **can't keep the secret to himself**, although he promised he would.

NASSOR

"Rise, Colossus, rise from your tomb!"

Nassor intends to **win th science fair** and **nothing will stop him**. Once he finds out about Victor's secret, he tries to **do the same with his departed pet**, a hamster called **Colossus**. The outcome isn't exactly what he was expecting.

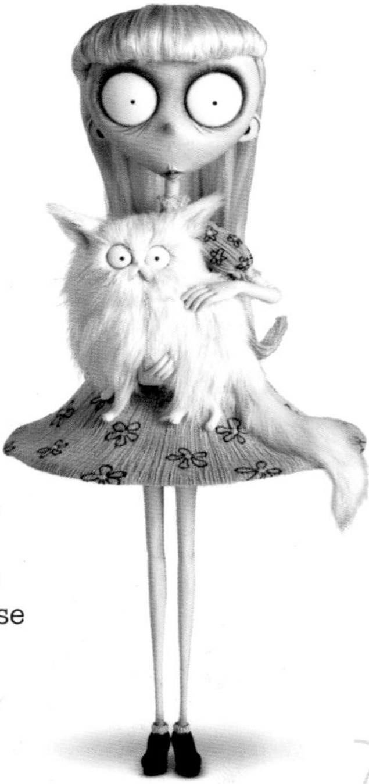

WEIRD GIRL

"It's an omen."

Weird girl is, well, **weird**. She spends most of her time with her beloved cat—**Mr. Whiskers**—and she is convinced he can sense when something big is about to happen to someone.

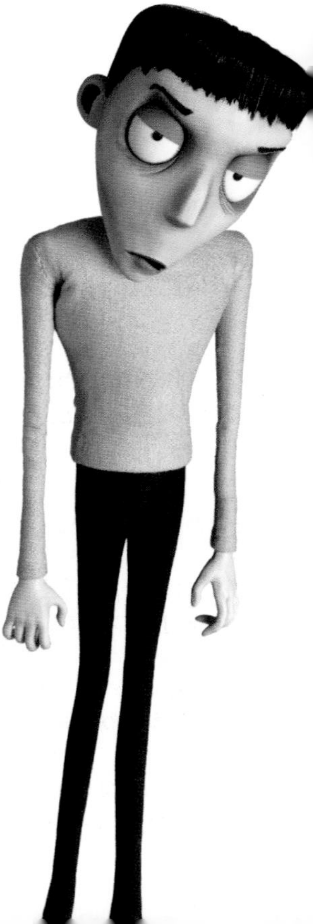

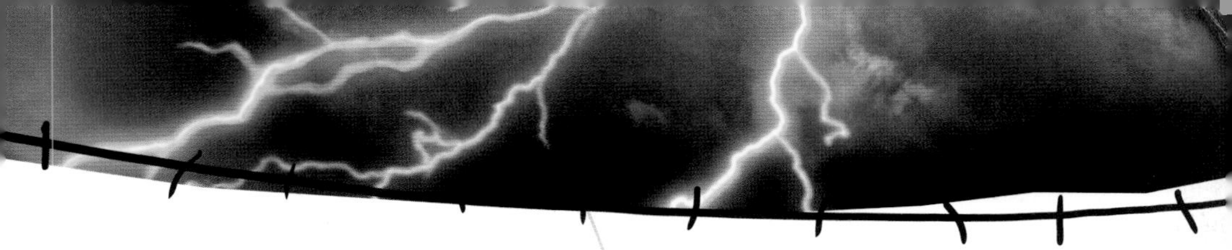

TOSHIAKI

"My problem's bigger!"

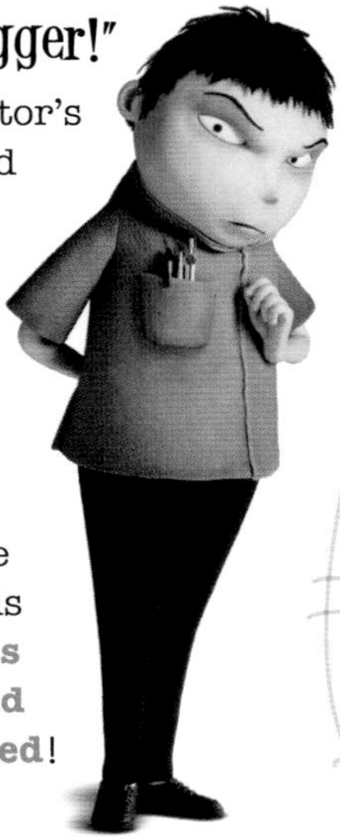

Just one look at Victor's attic chalkboard and Toshiaki uncovers the secret of his classmate's experiment. But his attempt to reproduce it **goes terribly wrong**: with a bottle of plant fertilizer, his beloved pet **becomes something he would have never imagined**!

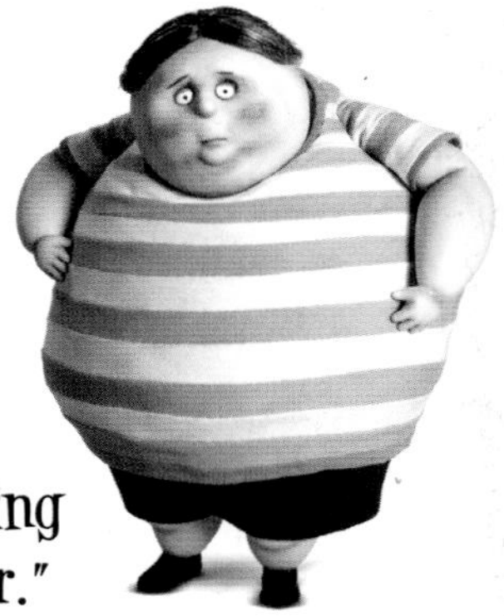

BOB

"We gotta come up with something better. Bigger."

Bob works with Toshiaki. He is his **friend**, **assistant** and, sometimes, **science victim**. Bob loves their science project, but when he discovers what Victor has been able to do, he knows they will have to work harder!

ELSA

"Do you know anything about science?"

Somber and **shy**, Elsa Van Helsing is **Victor's neighbor** and **classmate**. Elsa also has a beloved pet, her poodle Persephone, and truly empathizes with Victor when he loses Sparky.

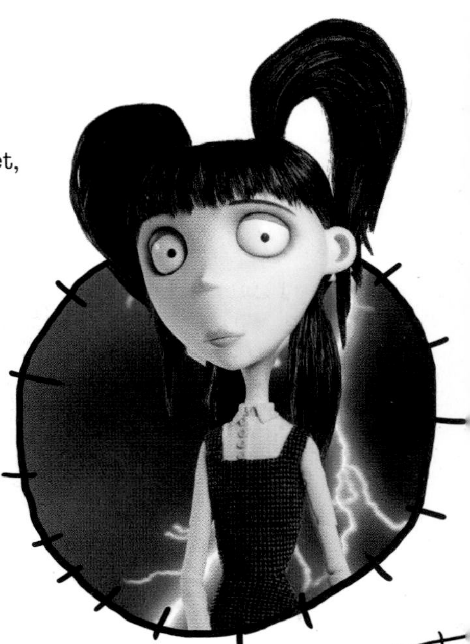

PERSEPHONE

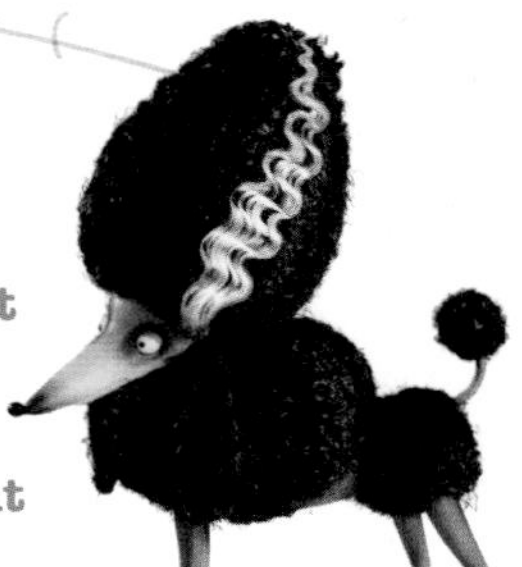

As Elsa's loyal dog, Persephone **gets to meet Sparky one day**. The attraction between the two is immediate: **love at first sight**. To her, bolts and sparks can only make Sparky more attractive!

"Science is not good or bad, Victor. But it can be used both ways. That is why you must always be careful."

MR. RZYKRUSKI

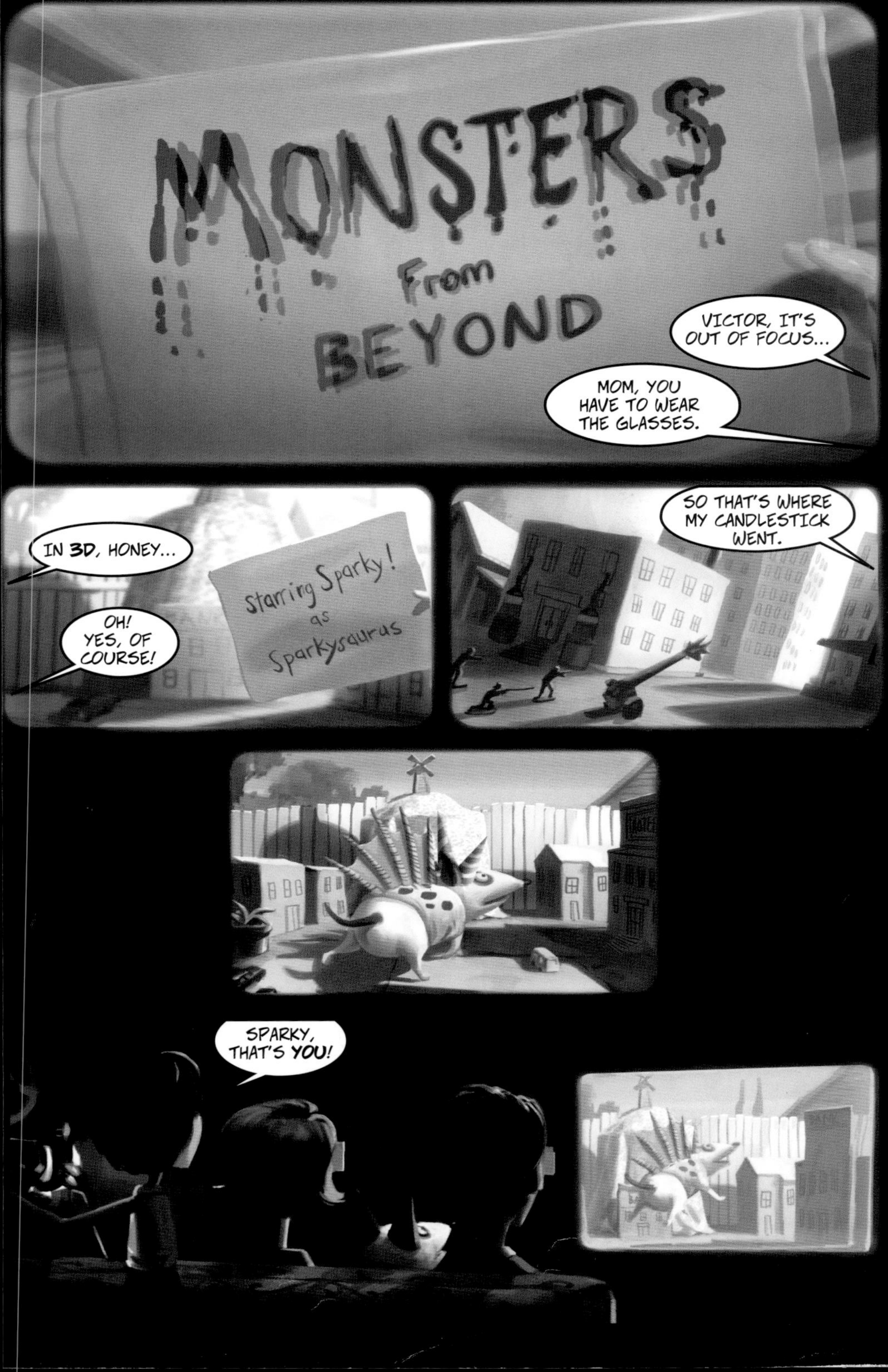
MONSTERS from BEYOND
VICTOR, IT'S OUT OF FOCUS...
MOM, YOU HAVE TO WEAR THE GLASSES.
IN 3D, HONEY...
OH! YES, OF COURSE!
starring Sparky! as Sparkysaurus
SO THAT'S WHERE MY CANDLESTICK WENT.
SPARKY, THAT'S YOU!

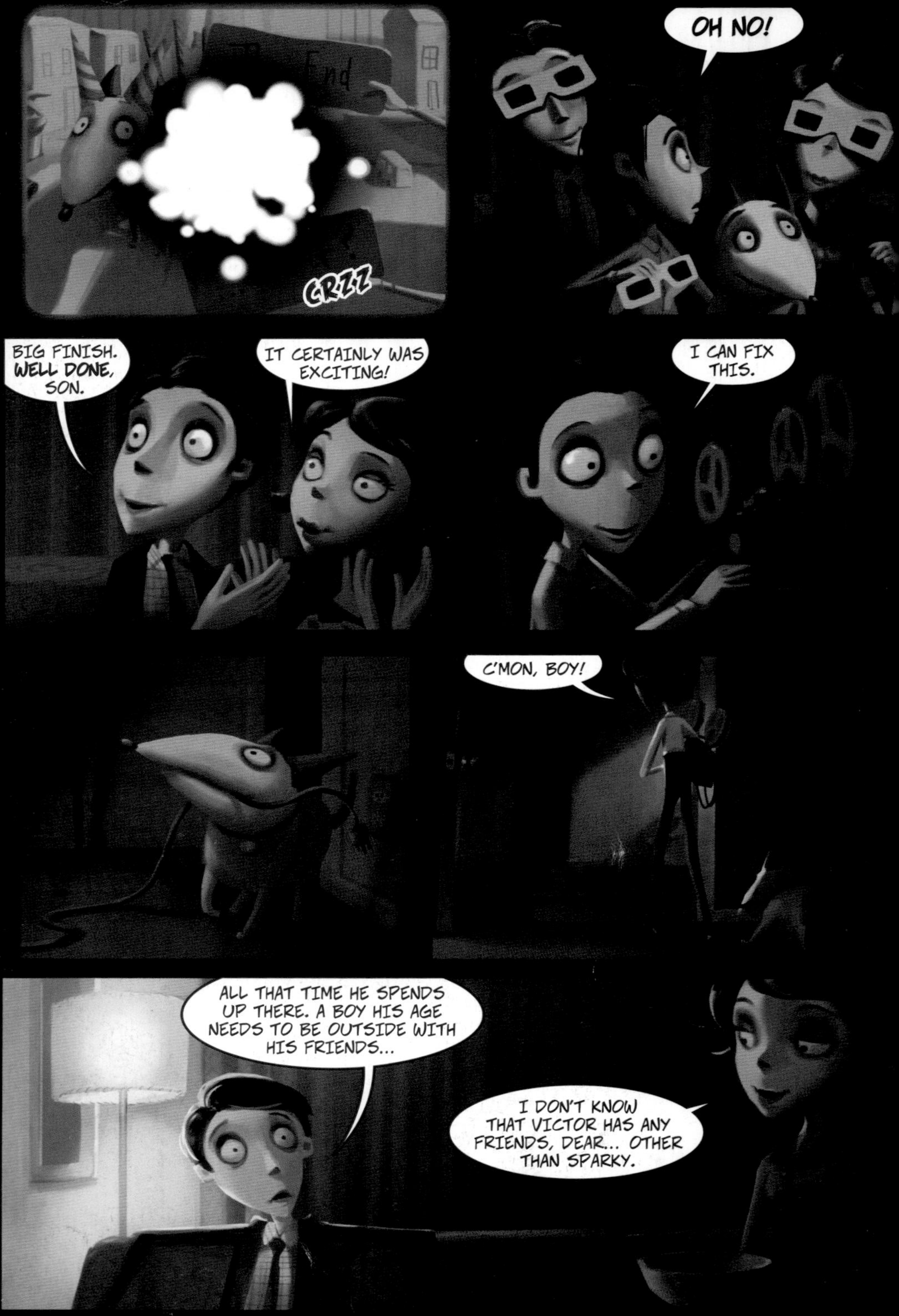
CRZZ
OH NO!
BIG FINISH. **WELL DONE,** SON.
IT CERTAINLY WAS EXCITING!
I CAN FIX THIS.
C'MON, BOY!
ALL THAT TIME HE SPENDS UP THERE. A BOY HIS AGE NEEDS TO BE OUTSIDE WITH HIS FRIENDS...
I DON'T KNOW THAT VICTOR HAS ANY FRIENDS, DEAR... OTHER THAN SPARKY.

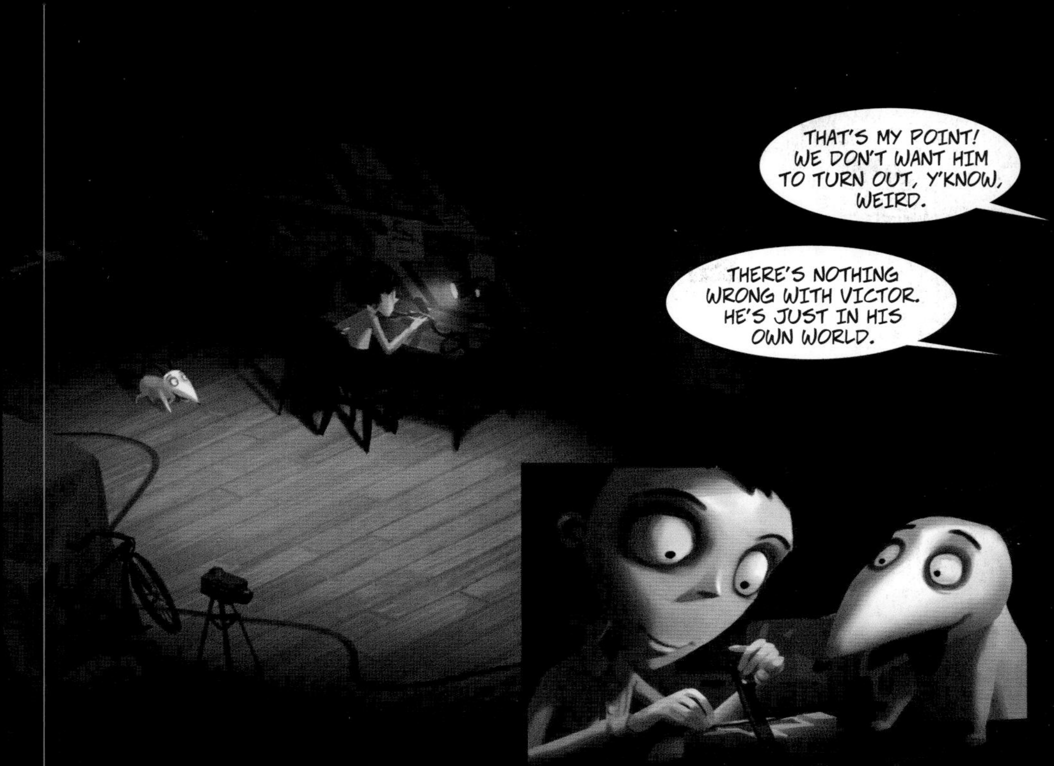
THAT'S MY POINT! WE DON'T WANT HIM TO TURN OUT, Y'KNOW, WEIRD.
THERE'S NOTHING WRONG WITH VICTOR. HE'S JUST IN HIS OWN WORLD.

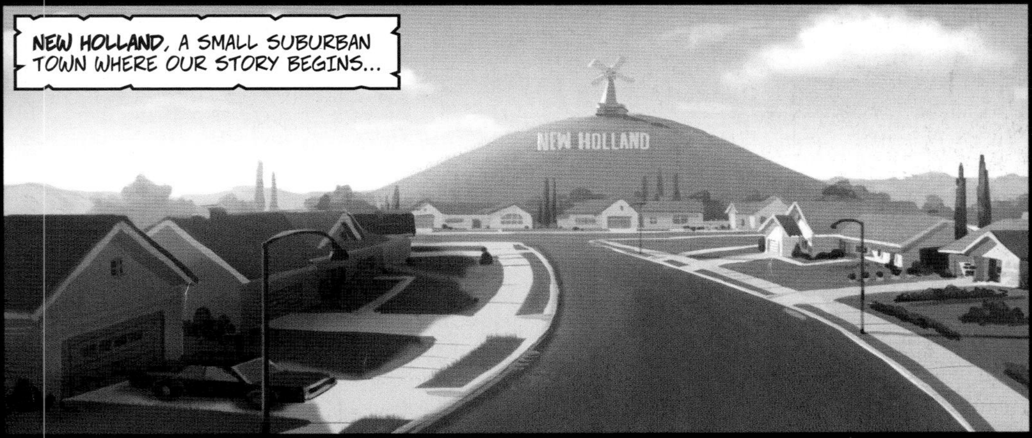
NEW HOLLAND, A SMALL SUBURBAN TOWN WHERE OUR STORY BEGINS...
NEW HOLLAND

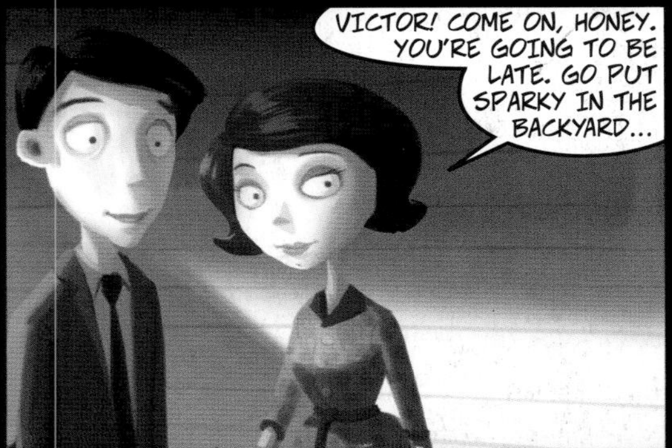
VICTOR! COME ON, HONEY. YOU'RE GOING TO BE LATE. GO PUT SPARKY IN THE BACKYARD...

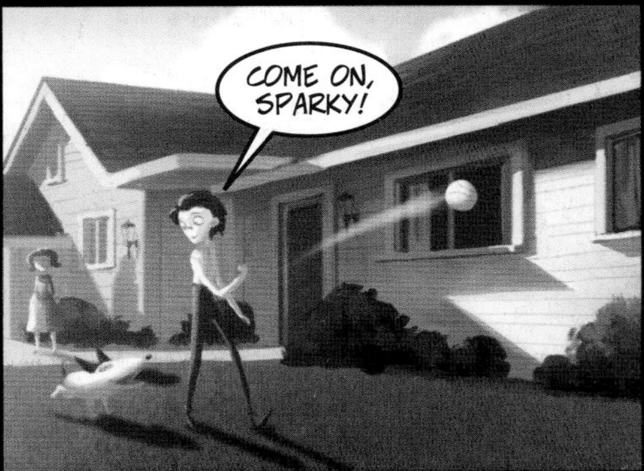
COME ON, SPARKY!

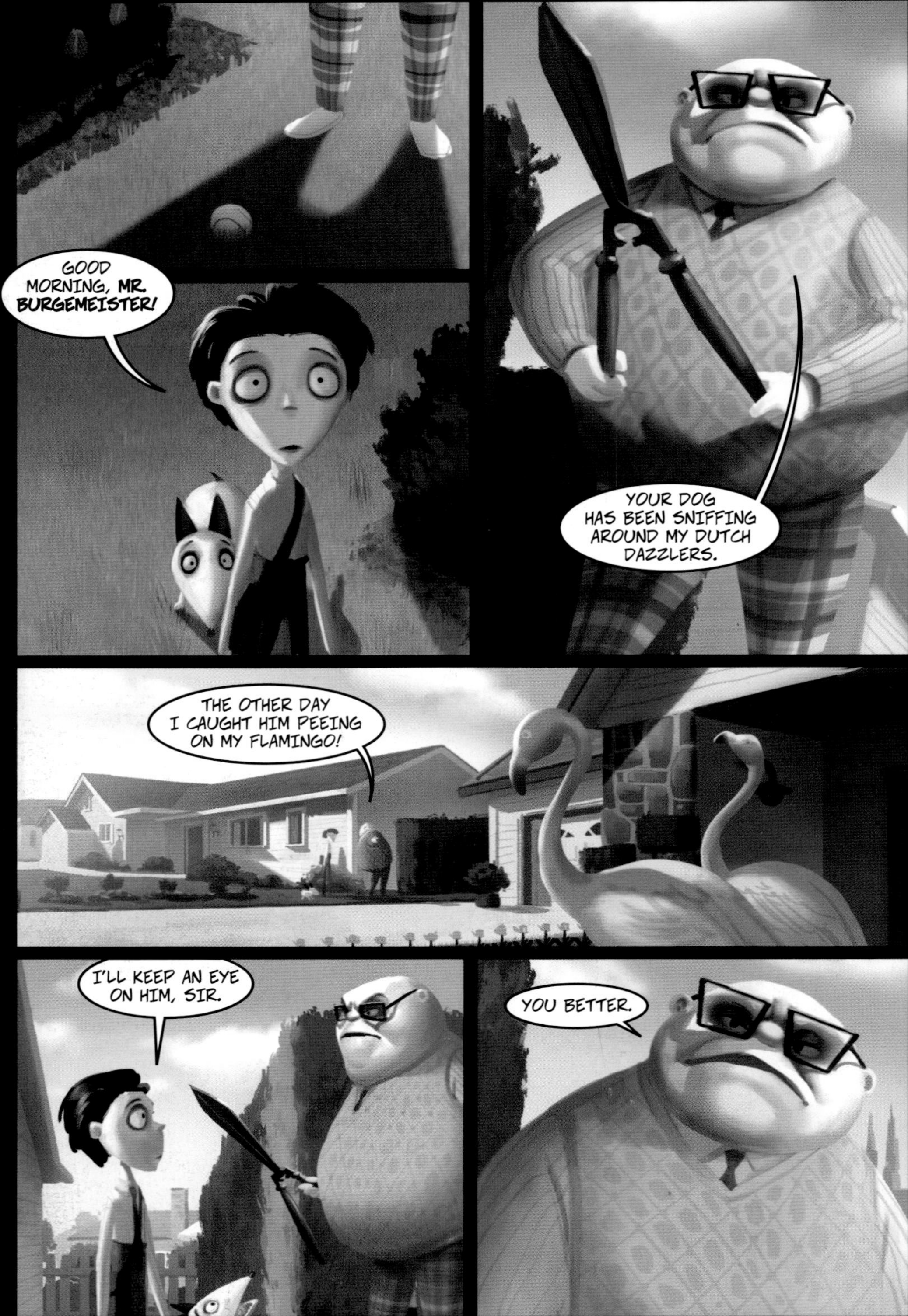
GOOD MORNING, MR. BURGEMEISTER!
YOUR DOG HAS BEEN SNIFFING AROUND MY DUTCH DAZZLERS.
THE OTHER DAY I CAUGHT HIM PEEING ON MY FLAMINGO!
I'LL KEEP AN EYE ON HIM, SIR.
YOU BETTER.

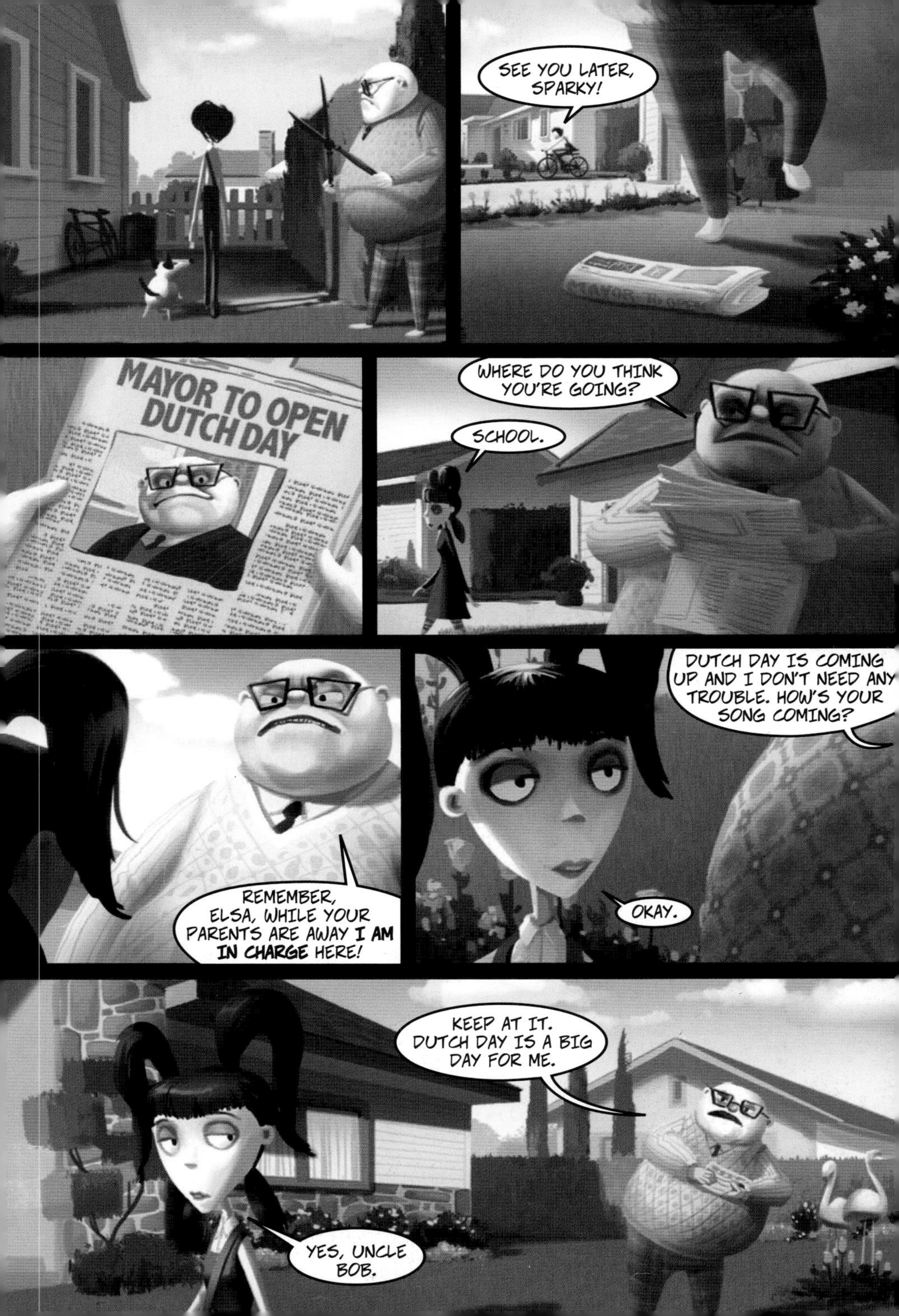
SEE YOU LATER, SPARKY!
MAYOR TO OPEN DUTCH DAY
WHERE DO YOU THINK YOU'RE GOING?
SCHOOL.
REMEMBER, ELSA, WHILE YOUR PARENTS ARE AWAY **I AM IN CHARGE** HERE!
DUTCH DAY IS COMING UP AND I DON'T NEED ANY TROUBLE. HOW'S YOUR SONG COMING?
OKAY.
KEEP AT IT. DUTCH DAY IS A BIG DAY FOR ME.
YES, UNCLE BOB.

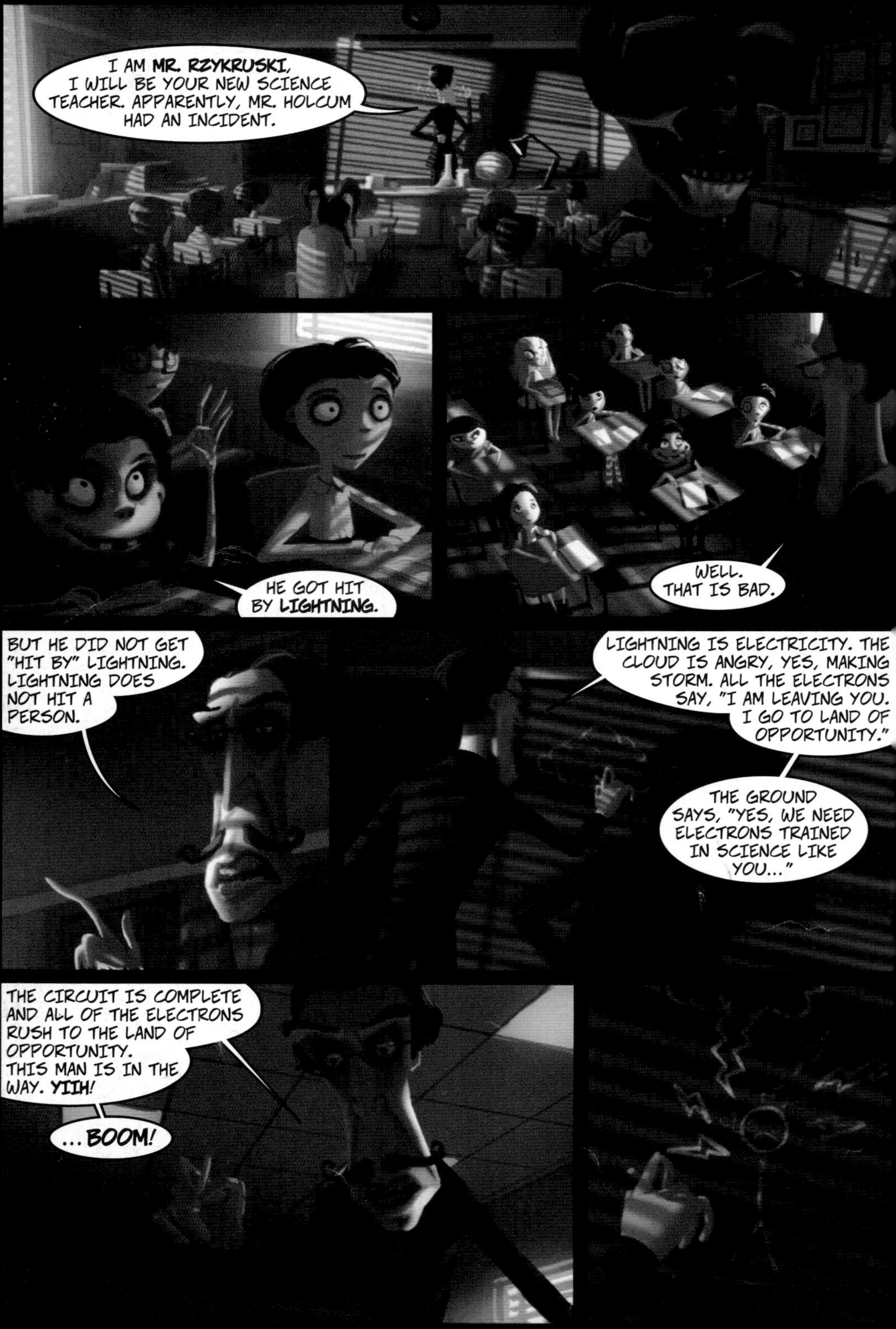
I AM **MR. RZYKRUSKI**, I WILL BE YOUR NEW SCIENCE TEACHER. APPARENTLY, MR. HOLCUM HAD AN INCIDENT.
HE GOT HIT BY **LIGHTNING**.
WELL. THAT IS BAD.
BUT HE DID NOT GET "HIT BY" LIGHTNING. LIGHTNING DOES NOT HIT A PERSON.
LIGHTNING IS ELECTRICITY. THE CLOUD IS ANGRY, YES, MAKING STORM. ALL THE ELECTRONS SAY, "I AM LEAVING YOU. I GO TO LAND OF OPPORTUNITY."
THE GROUND SAYS, "YES, WE NEED ELECTRONS TRAINED IN SCIENCE LIKE YOU..."
THE CIRCUIT IS COMPLETE AND ALL OF THE ELECTRONS RUSH TO THE LAND OF OPPORTUNITY. THIS MAN IS IN THE WAY. **YIIH!**
...BOOM!

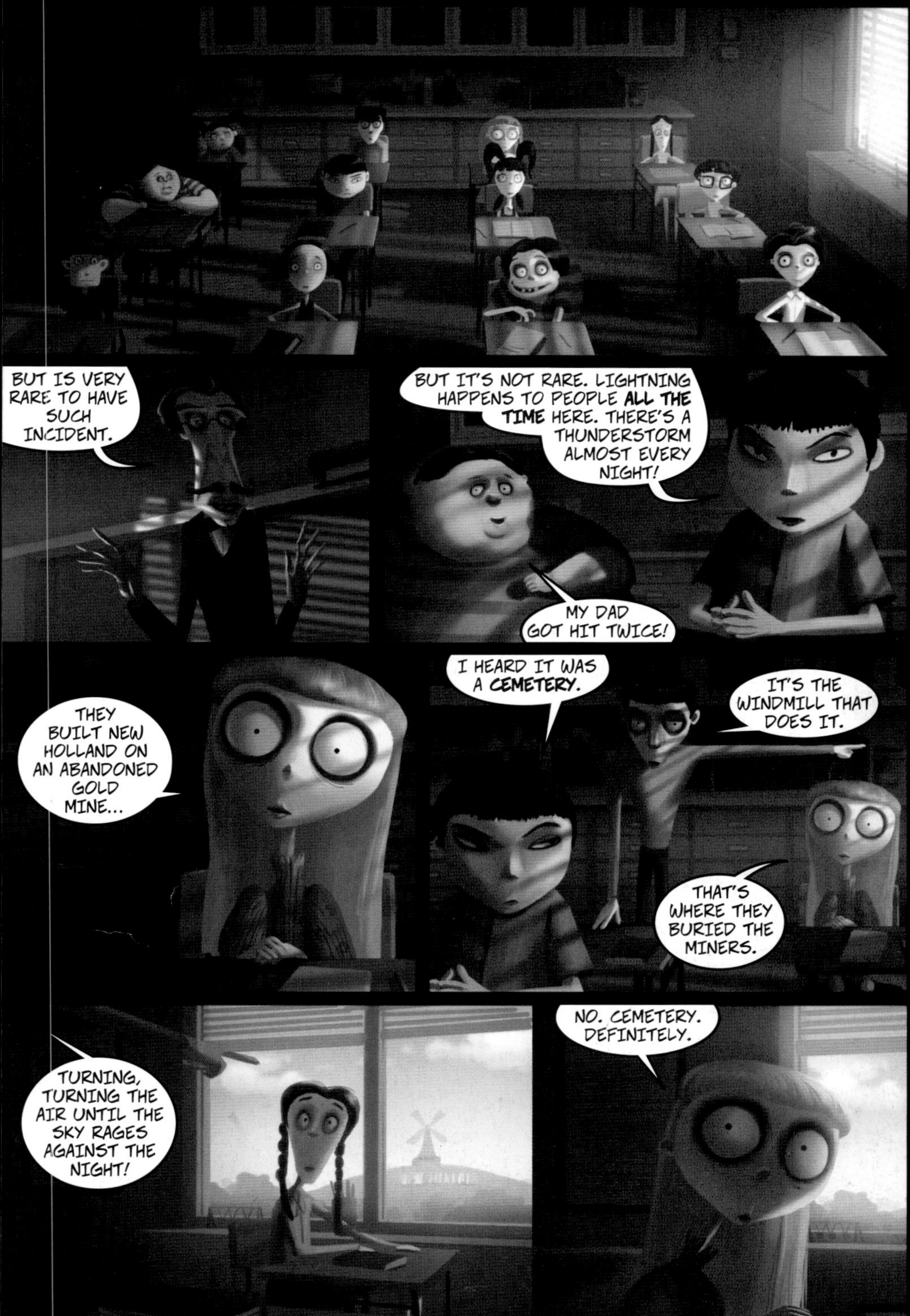

BUT IS VERY RARE TO HAVE SUCH INCIDENT.
BUT IT'S NOT RARE. LIGHTNING HAPPENS TO PEOPLE **ALL THE TIME** HERE. THERE'S A THUNDERSTORM ALMOST EVERY NIGHT!
MY DAD GOT HIT TWICE!
THEY BUILT NEW HOLLAND ON AN ABANDONED GOLD MINE...
I HEARD IT WAS A **CEMETERY**.
IT'S THE WINDMILL THAT DOES IT.
THAT'S WHERE THEY BURIED THE MINERS.
TURNING, TURNING THE AIR UNTIL THE SKY RAGES AGAINST THE NIGHT!
NO. CEMETERY. DEFINITELY.

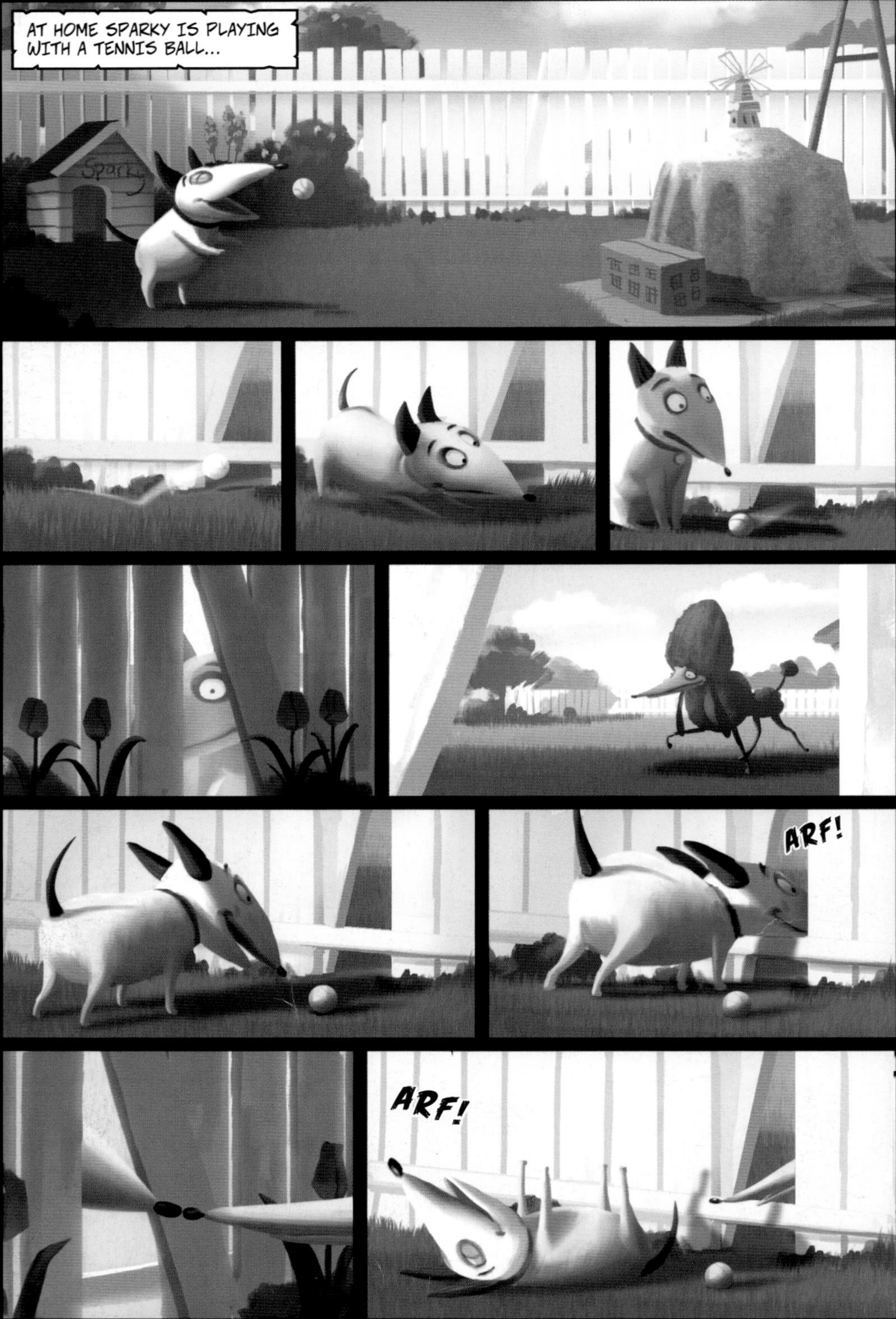
AT HOME SPARKY IS PLAYING WITH A TENNIS BALL...
Sparky
ARF!
ARF!

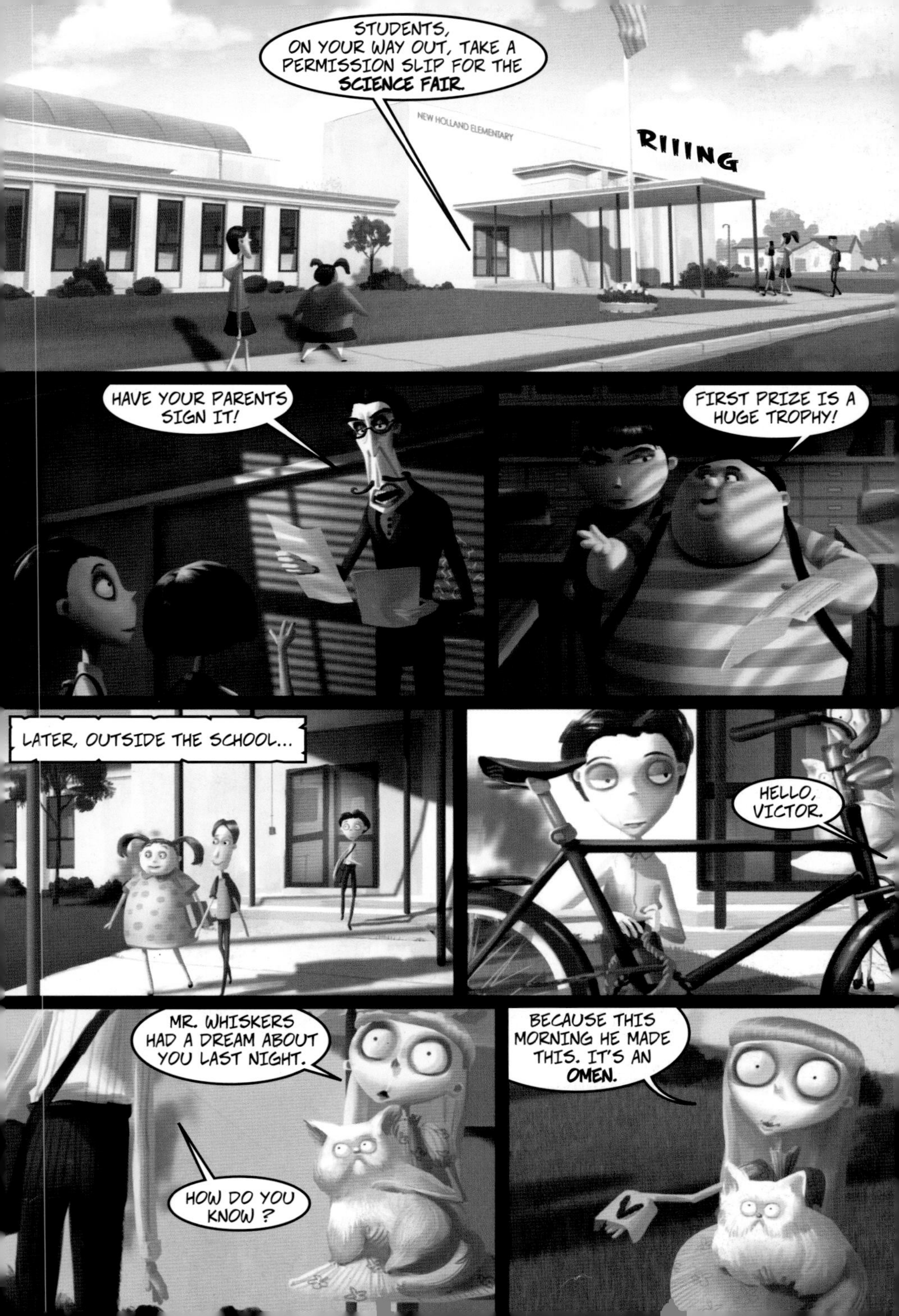
STUDENTS, ON YOUR WAY OUT, TAKE A PERMISSION SLIP FOR THE SCIENCE FAIR.
NEW HOLLAND ELEMENTARY
RIIING
HAVE YOUR PARENTS SIGN IT!
FIRST PRIZE IS A HUGE TROPHY!
LATER, OUTSIDE THE SCHOOL...
HELLO, VICTOR.
MR. WHISKERS HAD A DREAM ABOUT YOU LAST NIGHT.
HOW DO YOU KNOW ?
BECAUSE THIS MORNING HE MADE THIS. IT'S AN OMEN.

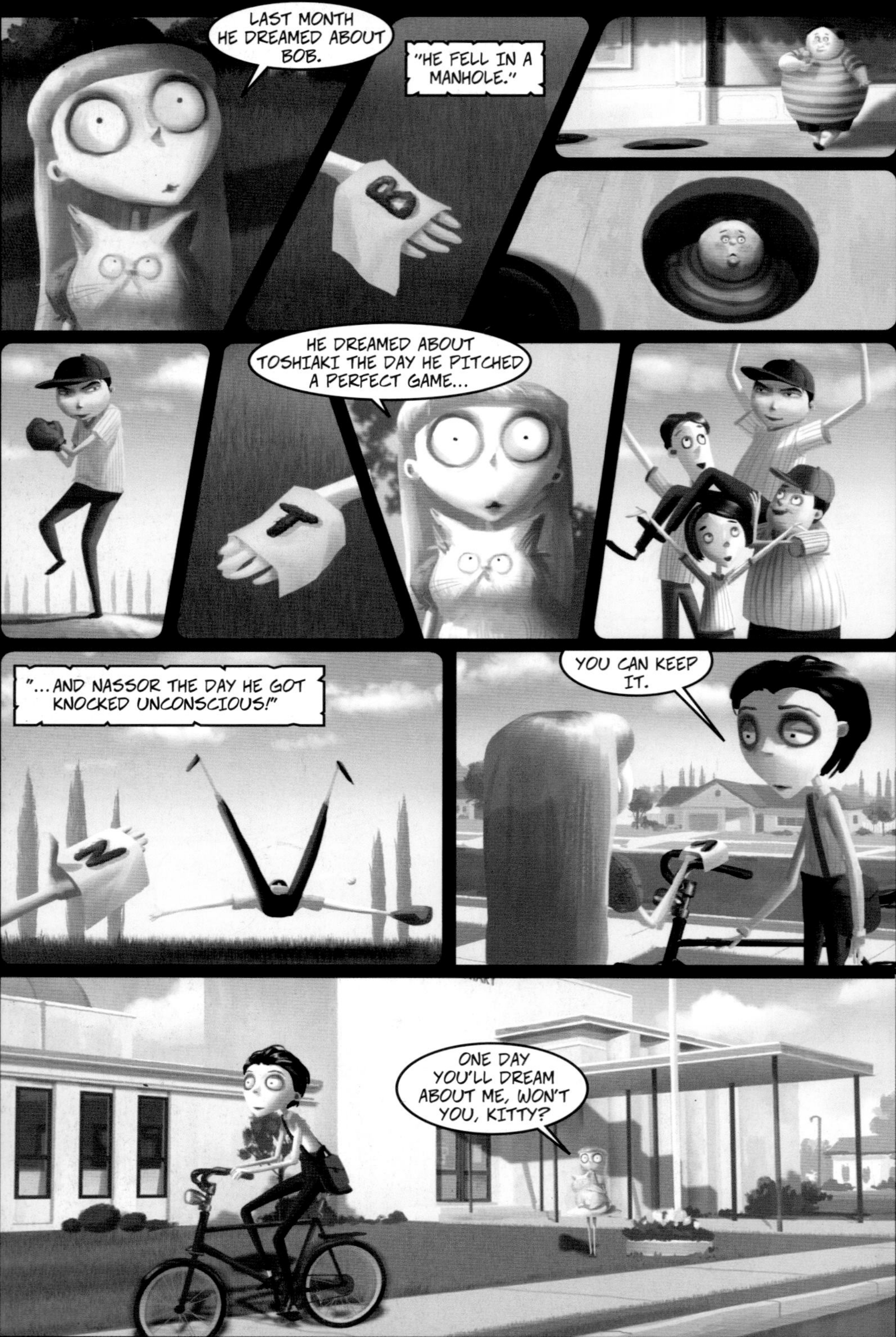
LAST MONTH HE DREAMED ABOUT BOB.
"HE FELL IN A MANHOLE."
HE DREAMED ABOUT TOSHIAKI THE DAY HE PITCHED A PERFECT GAME...
"...AND NASSOR THE DAY HE GOT KNOCKED UNCONSCIOUS!"
YOU CAN KEEP IT.
ONE DAY YOU'LL DREAM ABOUT ME, WON'T YOU, KITTY?

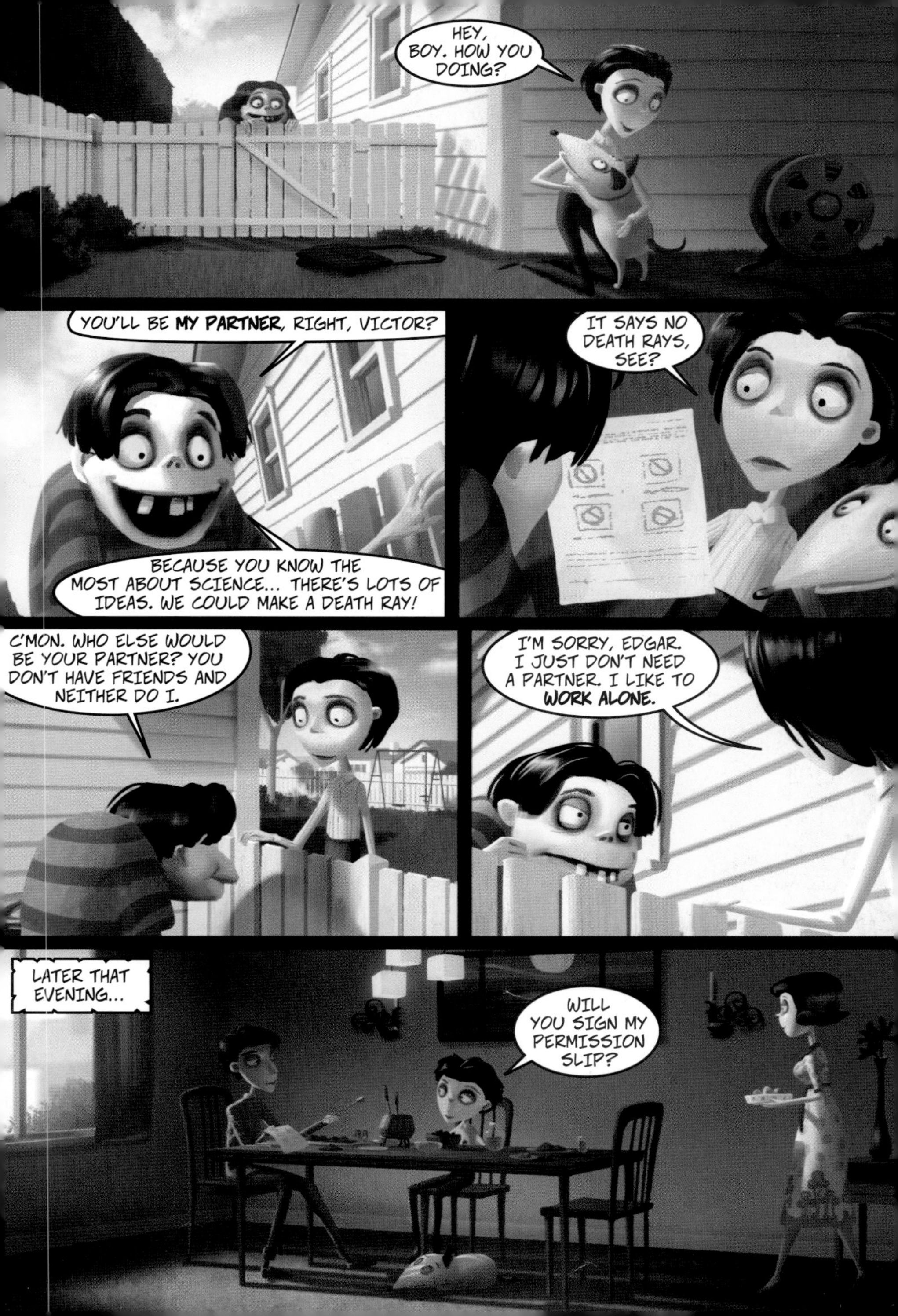
HEY, BOY. HOW YOU DOING?
YOU'LL BE **MY PARTNER**, RIGHT, VICTOR?
BECAUSE YOU KNOW THE MOST ABOUT SCIENCE... THERE'S LOTS OF IDEAS. WE COULD MAKE A DEATH RAY!
IT SAYS NO DEATH RAYS, SEE?
C'MON. WHO ELSE WOULD BE YOUR PARTNER? YOU DON'T HAVE FRIENDS AND NEITHER DO I.
I'M SORRY, EDGAR. I JUST DON'T NEED A PARTNER. I LIKE TO **WORK ALONE.**
LATER THAT EVENING...
WILL YOU SIGN MY PERMISSION SLIP?

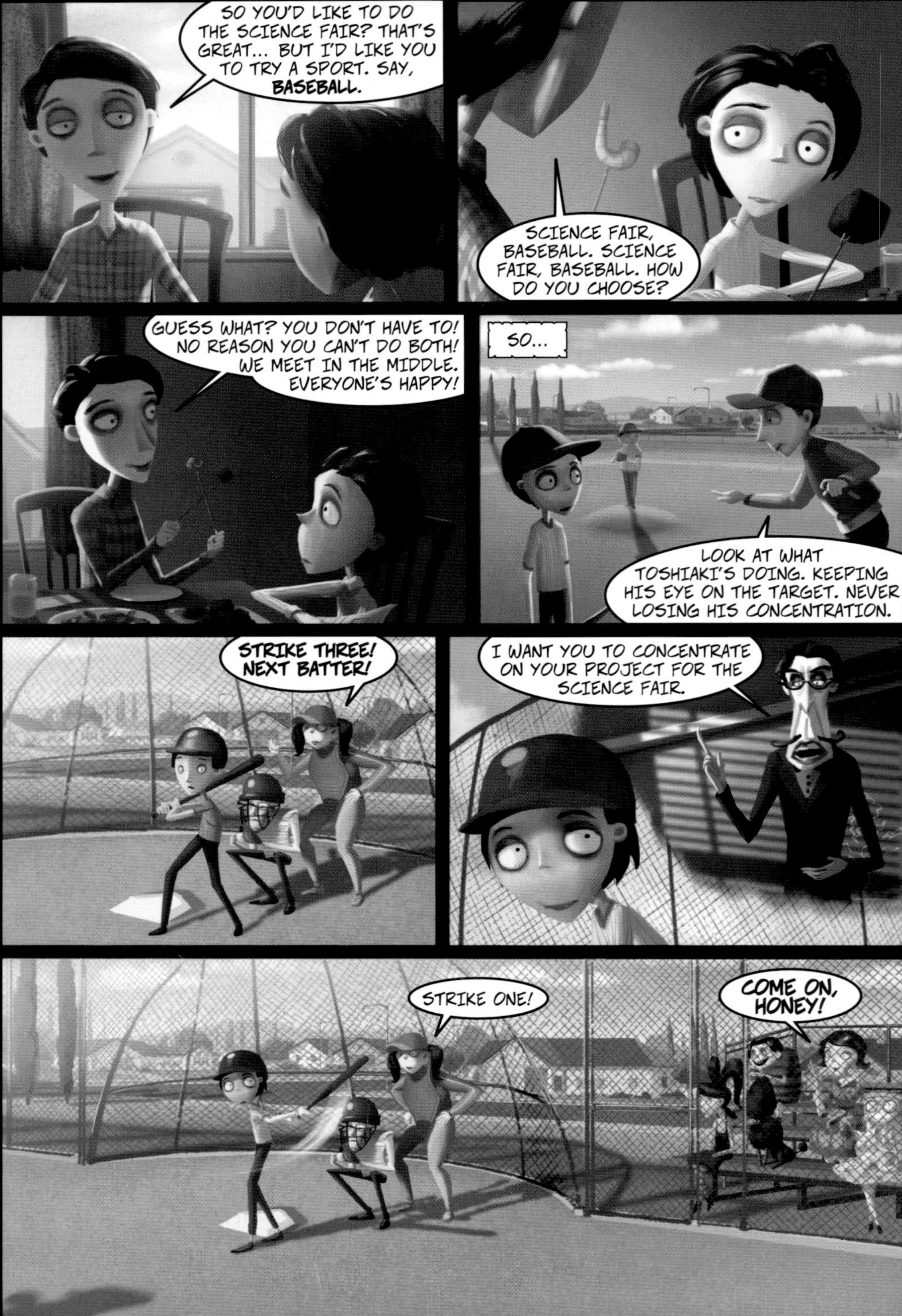

SO YOU'D LIKE TO DO THE SCIENCE FAIR? THAT'S GREAT... BUT I'D LIKE YOU TO TRY A SPORT. SAY, **BASEBALL.**
SCIENCE FAIR, BASEBALL. SCIENCE FAIR, BASEBALL. HOW DO YOU CHOOSE?
GUESS WHAT? YOU DON'T HAVE TO! NO REASON YOU CAN'T DO BOTH! WE MEET IN THE MIDDLE. EVERYONE'S HAPPY!
SO...
LOOK AT WHAT TOSHIAKI'S DOING. KEEPING HIS EYE ON THE TARGET. NEVER LOSING HIS CONCENTRATION.
STRIKE THREE! NEXT BATTER!
I WANT YOU TO CONCENTRATE ON YOUR PROJECT FOR THE SCIENCE FAIR.
STRIKE ONE!
COME ON, HONEY!

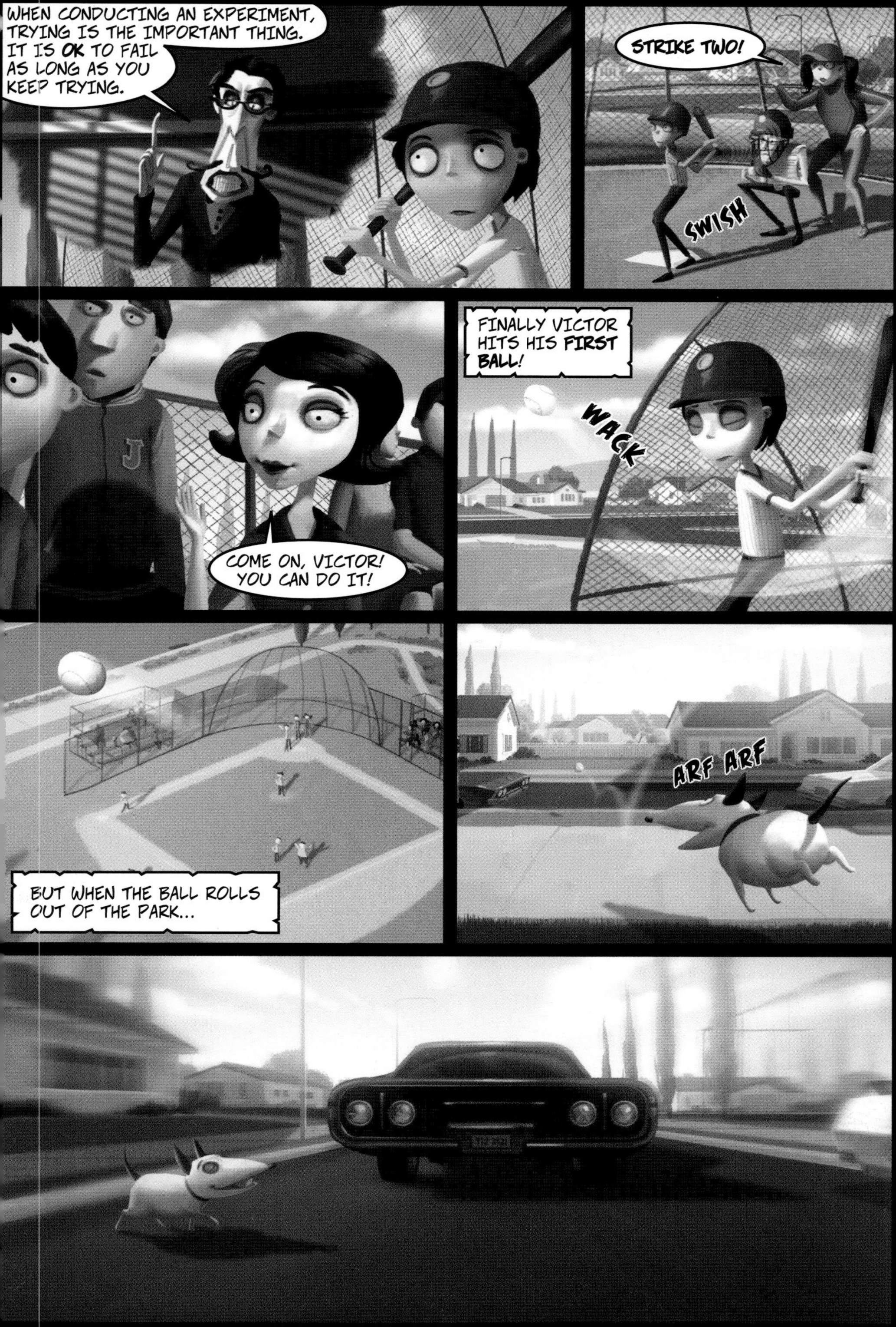
WHEN CONDUCTING AN EXPERIMENT, TRYING IS THE IMPORTANT THING. IT IS **OK** TO FAIL AS LONG AS YOU KEEP TRYING.
STRIKE TWO!
SWISH
COME ON, VICTOR! YOU CAN DO IT!
FINALLY VICTOR HITS HIS **FIRST BALL**!
WACK
BUT WHEN THE BALL ROLLS OUT OF THE PARK...
ARF ARF

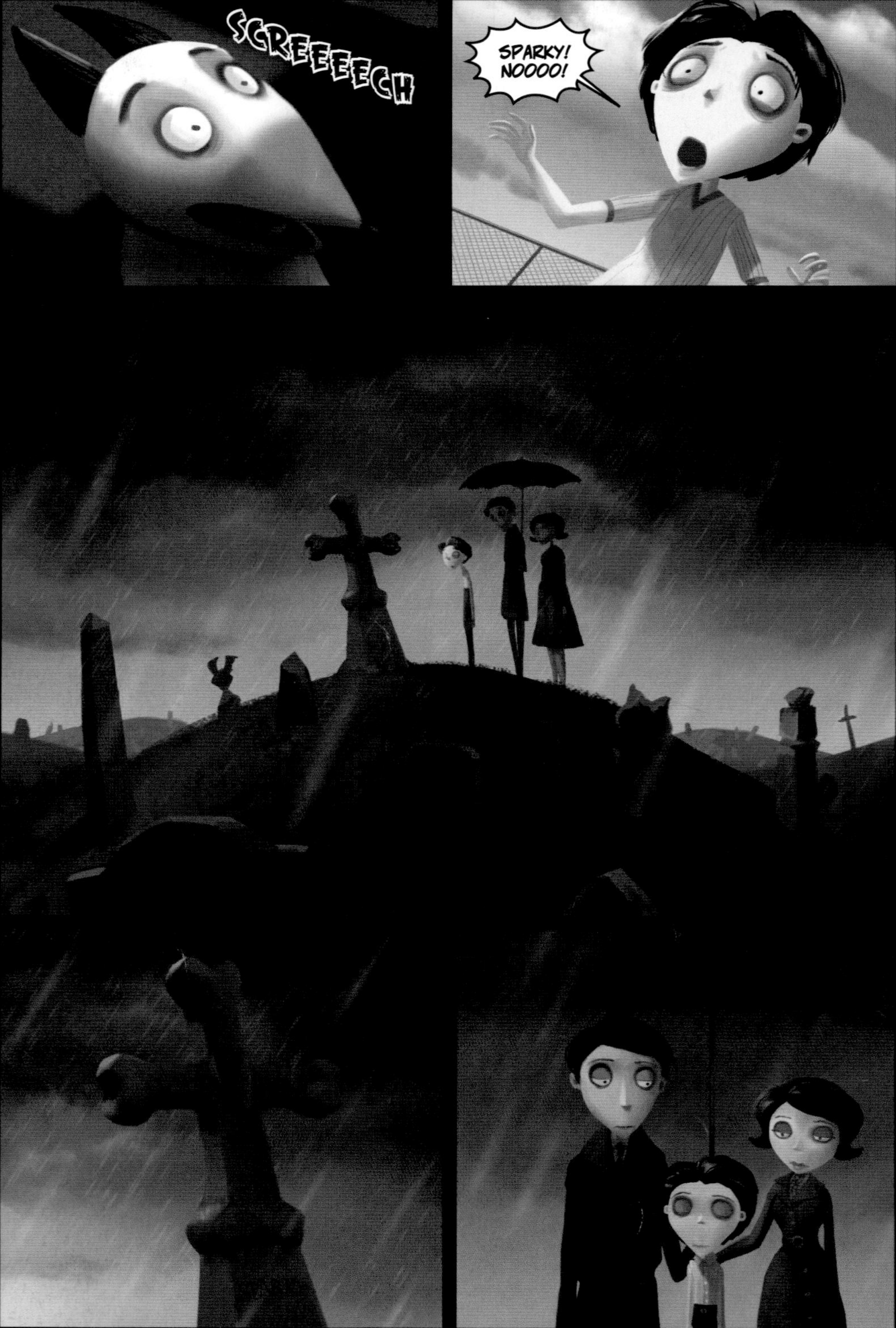
SCREEEEECH
SPARKY! NOOOO!

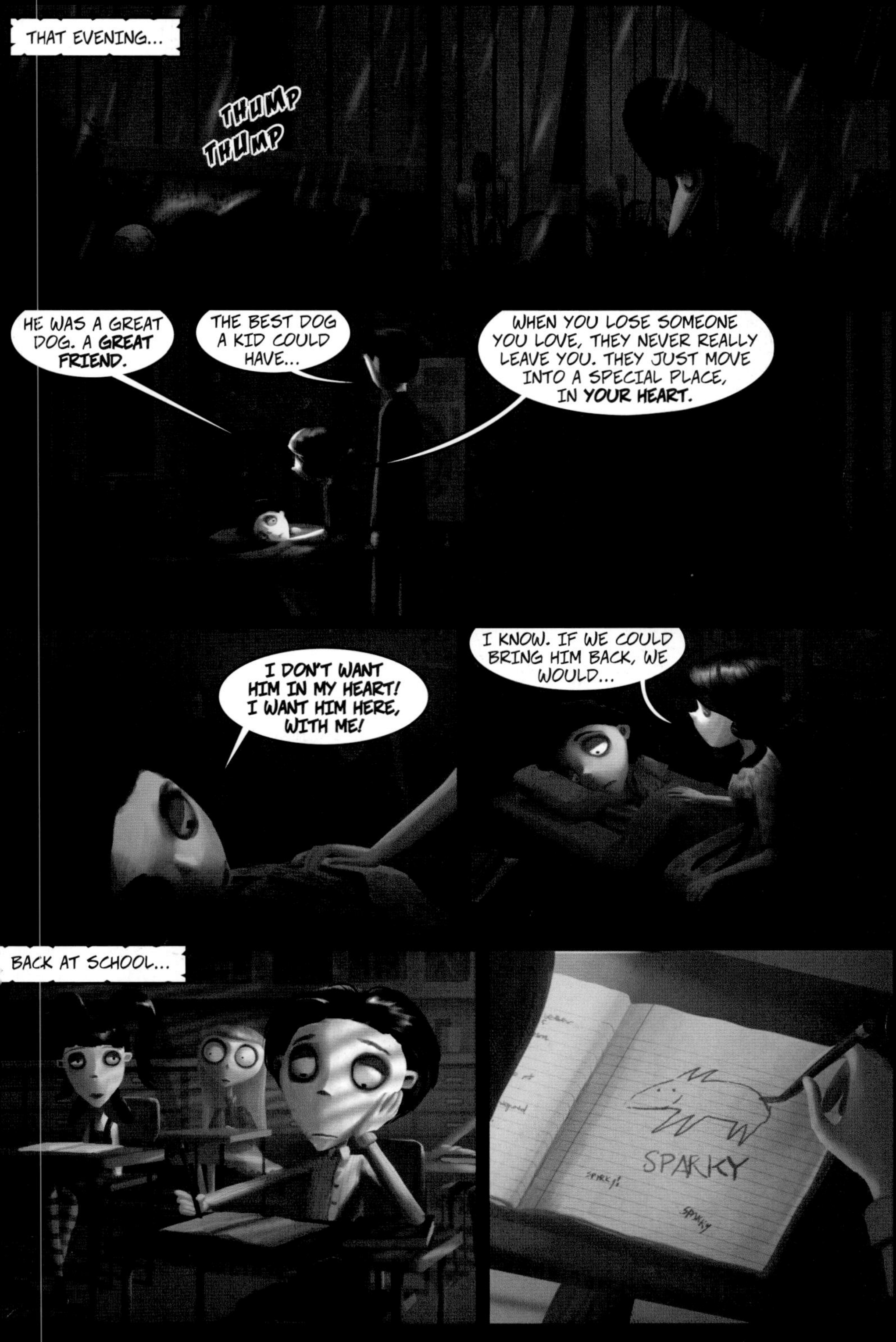
THAT EVENING...
THUMP THUMP
HE WAS A GREAT DOG. A **GREAT FRIEND**.
THE BEST DOG A KID COULD HAVE...
WHEN YOU LOSE SOMEONE YOU LOVE, THEY NEVER REALLY LEAVE YOU. THEY JUST MOVE INTO A SPECIAL PLACE, IN **YOUR HEART**.
I DON'T WANT HIM IN MY HEART! I WANT HIM HERE, WITH ME!
I KNOW. IF WE COULD BRING HIM BACK, WE WOULD...
BACK AT SCHOOL...
SPARKY

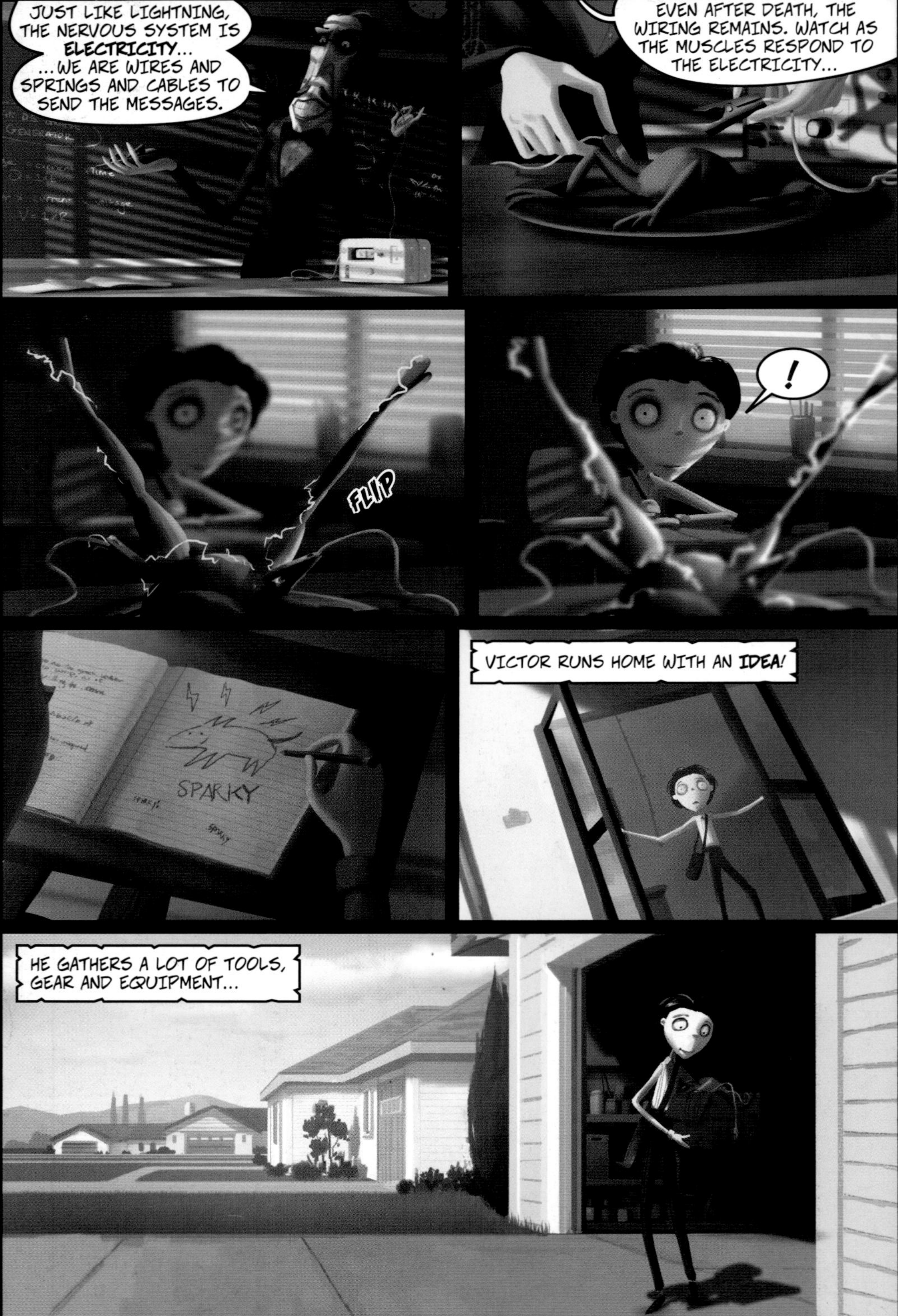
JUST LIKE LIGHTNING, THE NERVOUS SYSTEM IS **ELECTRICITY**... ...WE ARE WIRES AND SPRINGS AND CABLES TO SEND THE MESSAGES.
EVEN AFTER DEATH, THE WIRING REMAINS. WATCH AS THE MUSCLES RESPOND TO THE ELECTRICITY...
FLIP
!
SPARKY
VICTOR RUNS HOME WITH AN **IDEA**!
HE GATHERS A LOT OF TOOLS, GEAR AND EQUIPMENT...

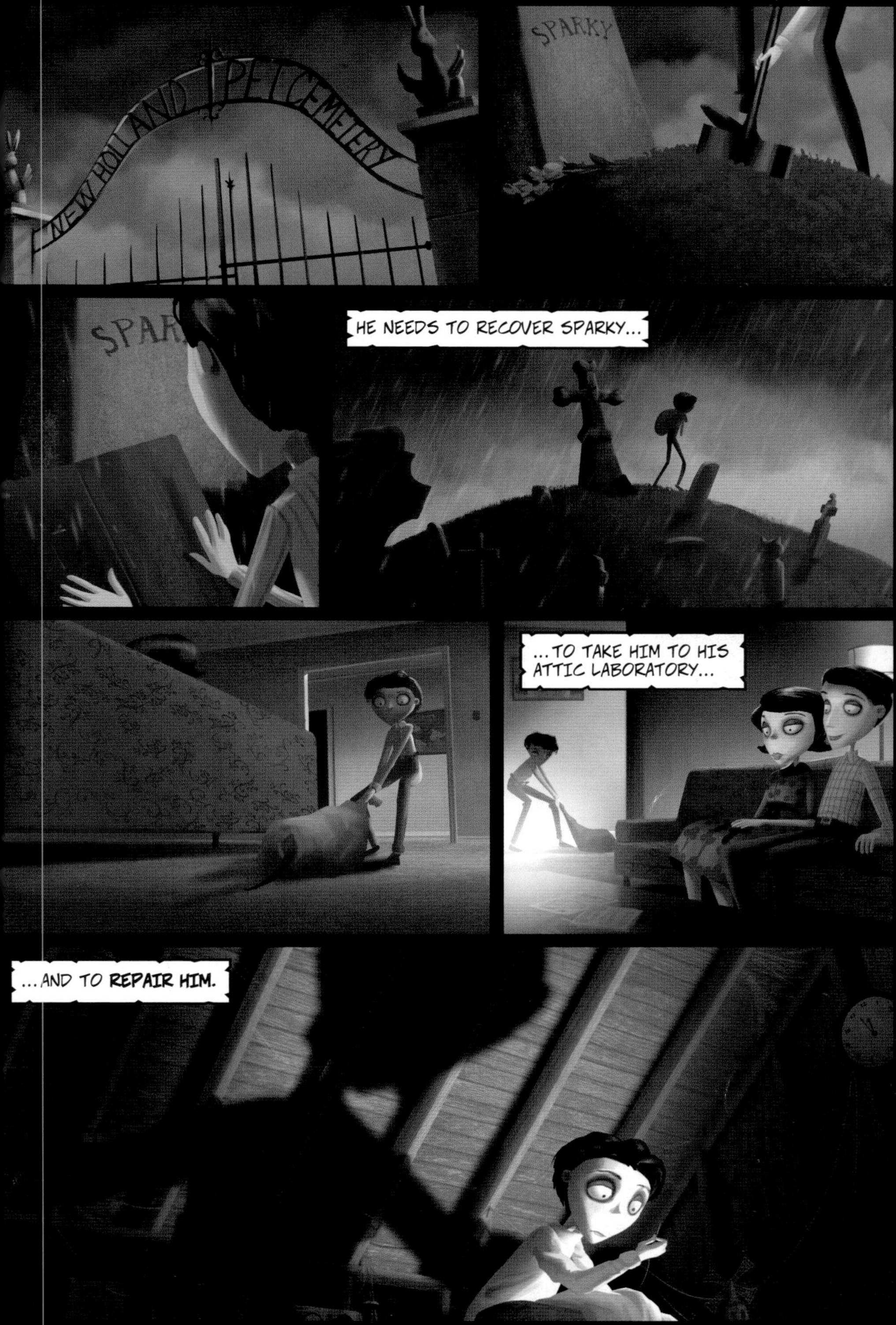
NEW HOLLAND PET CEMETERY
SPARKY
SPARKY
HE NEEDS TO RECOVER SPARKY...
...TO TAKE HIM TO HIS ATTIC LABORATORY...
...AND TO REPAIR HIM.

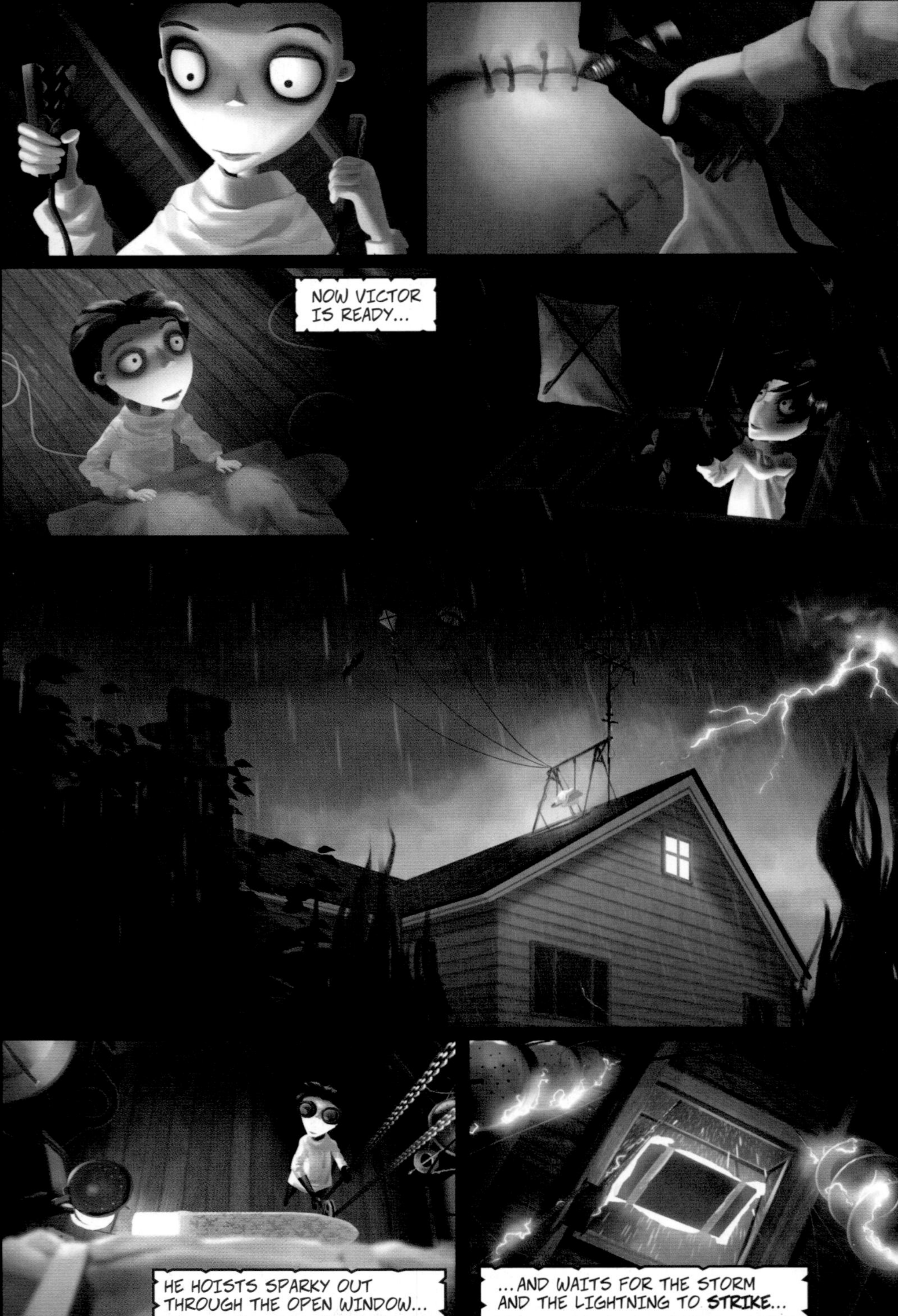
NOW VICTOR IS READY...
HE HOISTS SPARKY OUT THROUGH THE OPEN WINDOW...
...AND WAITS FOR THE STORM AND THE LIGHTNING TO **STRIKE**...

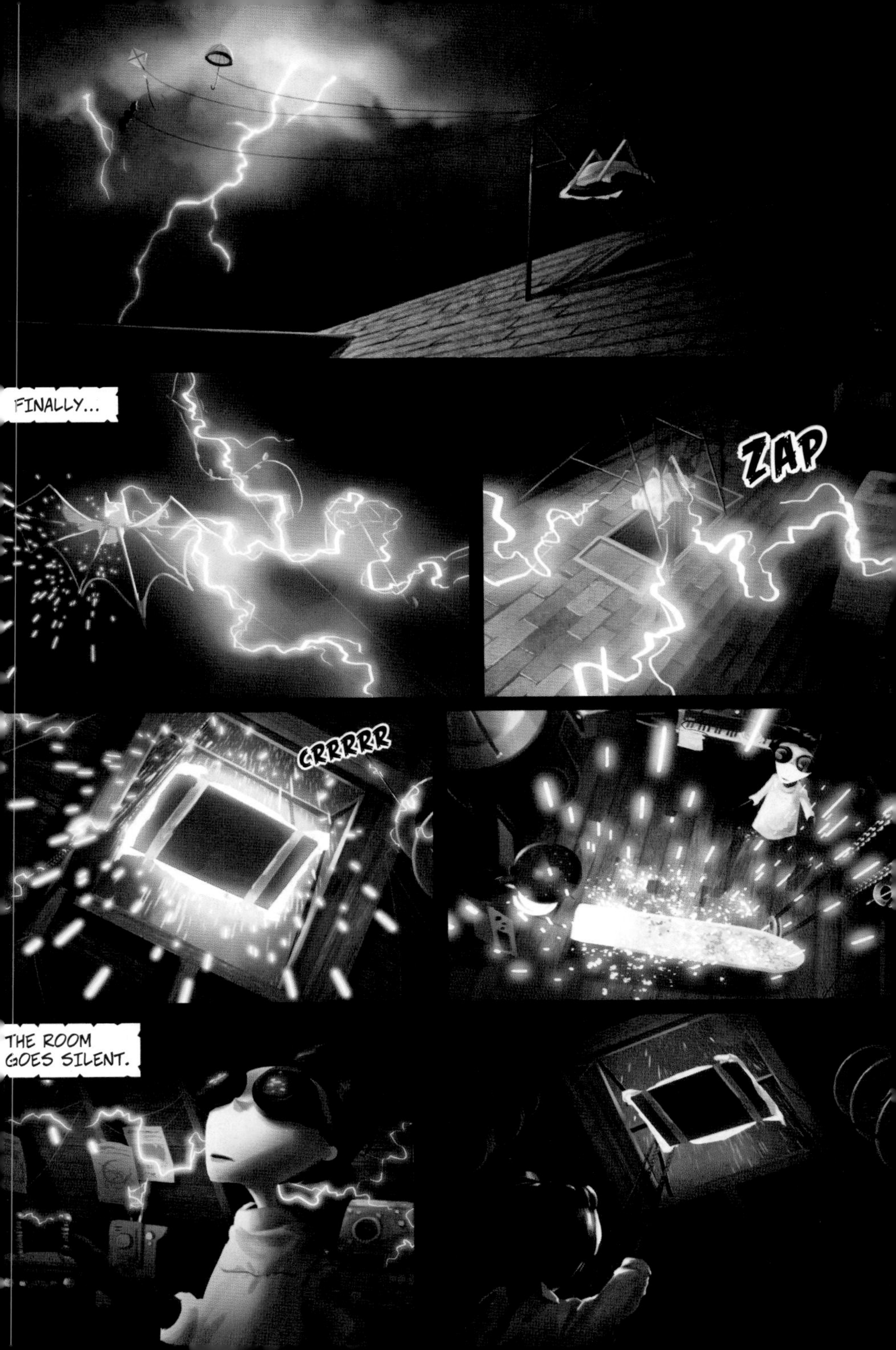
FINALLY...
ZAP
CRRRRR
THE ROOM GOES SILENT.

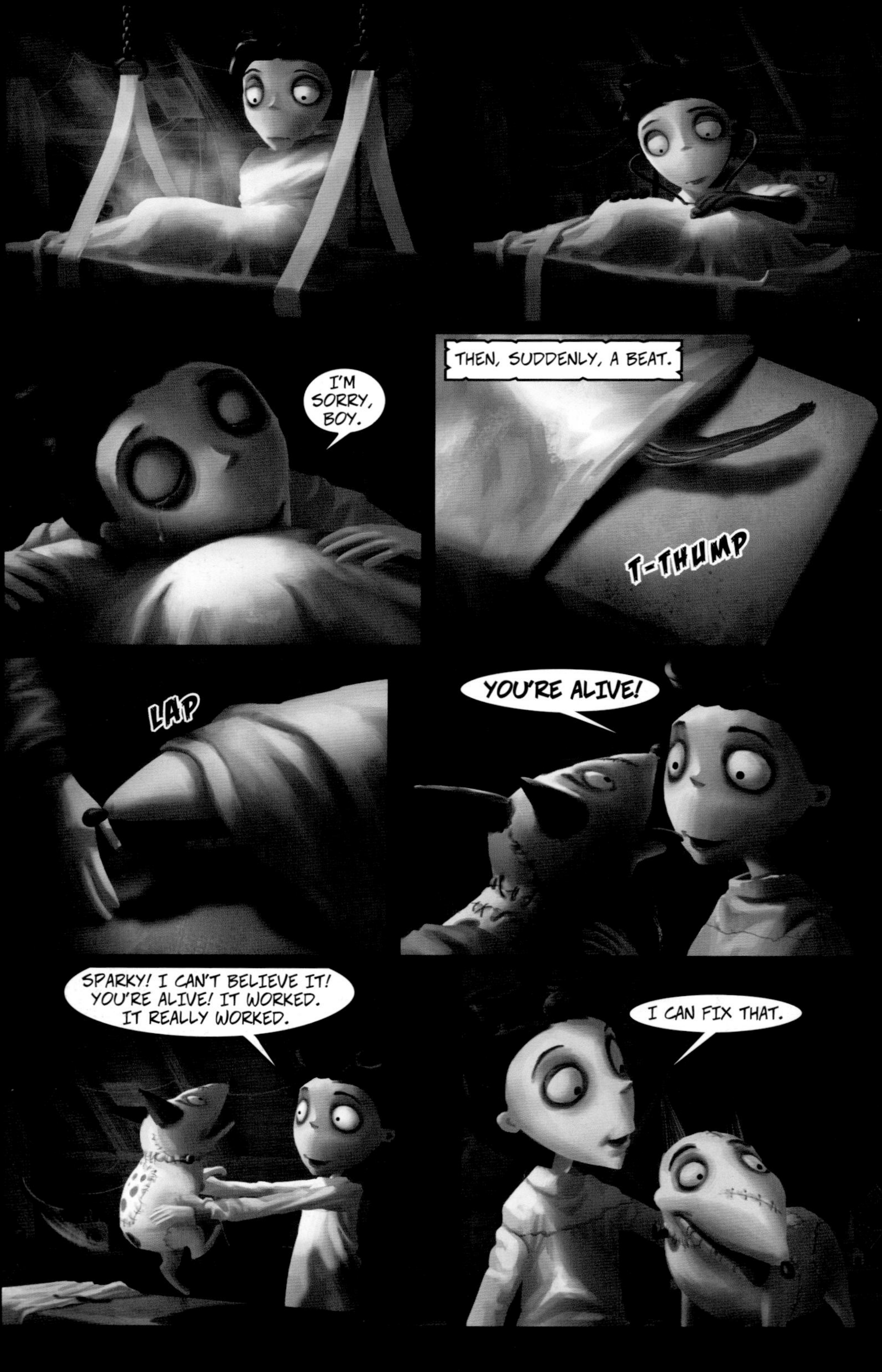
I'M SORRY, BOY.
THEN, SUDDENLY, A BEAT.
T-THUMP
LAP
YOU'RE ALIVE!
SPARKY! I CAN'T BELIEVE IT! YOU'RE ALIVE! IT WORKED. IT REALLY WORKED.
I CAN FIX THAT.

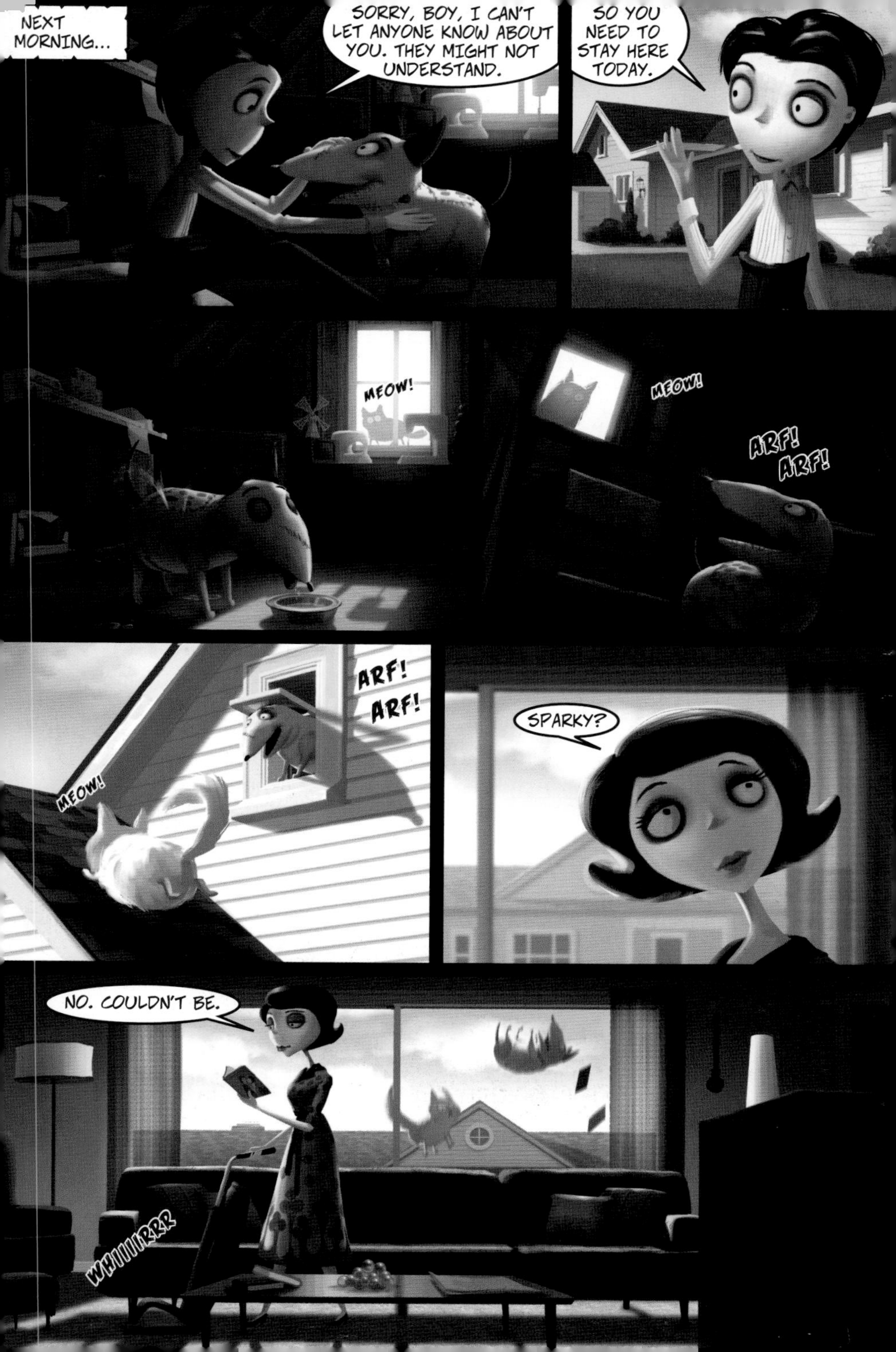
NEXT MORNING...
SORRY, BOY, I CAN'T LET ANYONE KNOW ABOUT YOU. THEY MIGHT NOT UNDERSTAND.
SO YOU NEED TO STAY HERE TODAY.
MEOW!
MEOW!
ARF! ARF!
ARF! ARF!
MEOW!
SPARKY?
NO. COULDN'T BE.
WHIIIIIRRR

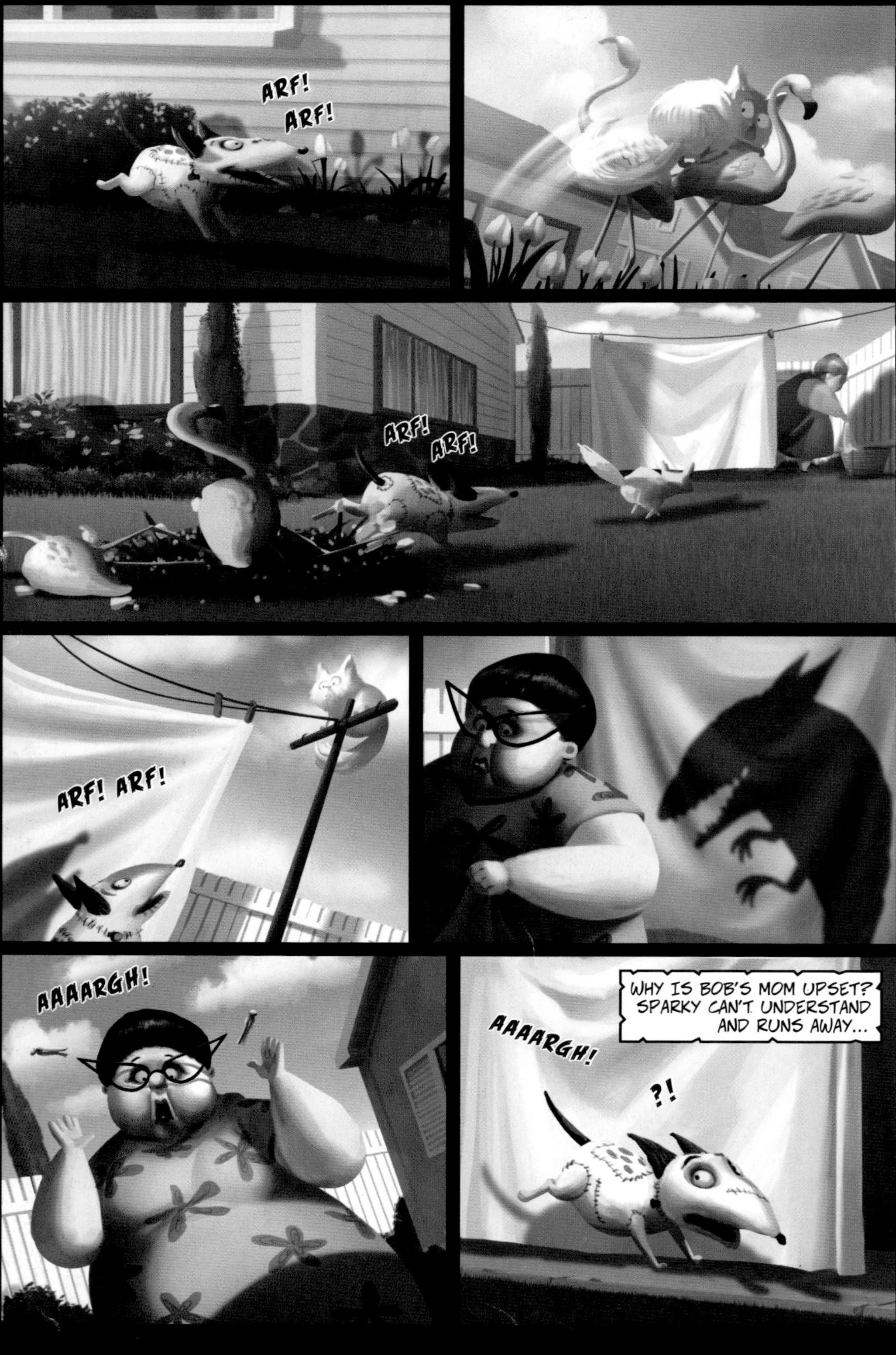
ARF!
ARF!
ARF!
ARF!
ARF! ARF!
AAAARGH!
WHY IS BOB'S MOM UPSET? SPARKY CAN'T UNDERSTAND AND RUNS AWAY...
AAAARGH!
?!

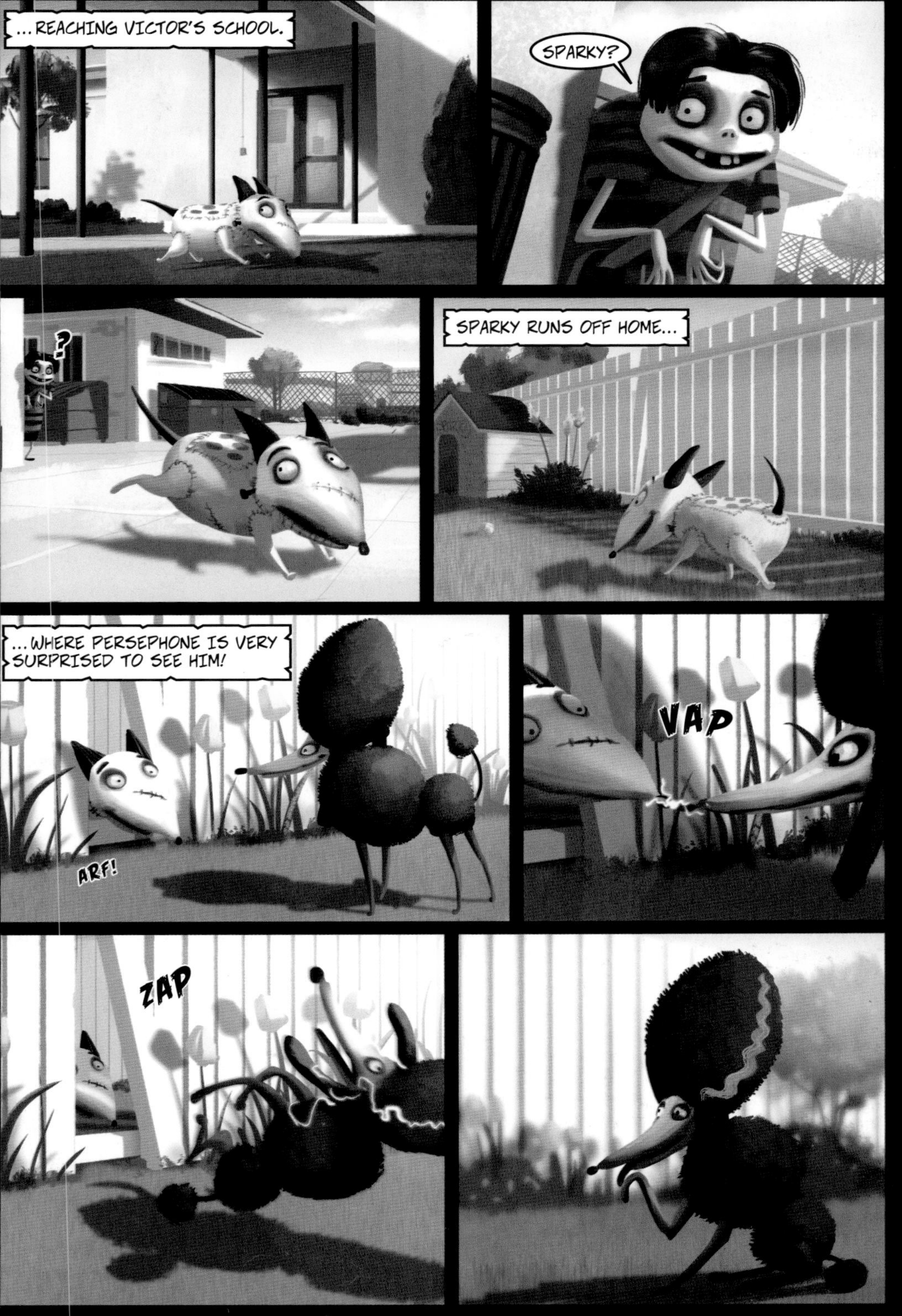
...REACHING VICTOR'S SCHOOL.
SPARKY?
?
SPARKY RUNS OFF HOME...
...WHERE PERSEPHONE IS VERY SURPRISED TO SEE HIM!
ARF!
VAP
ZAP

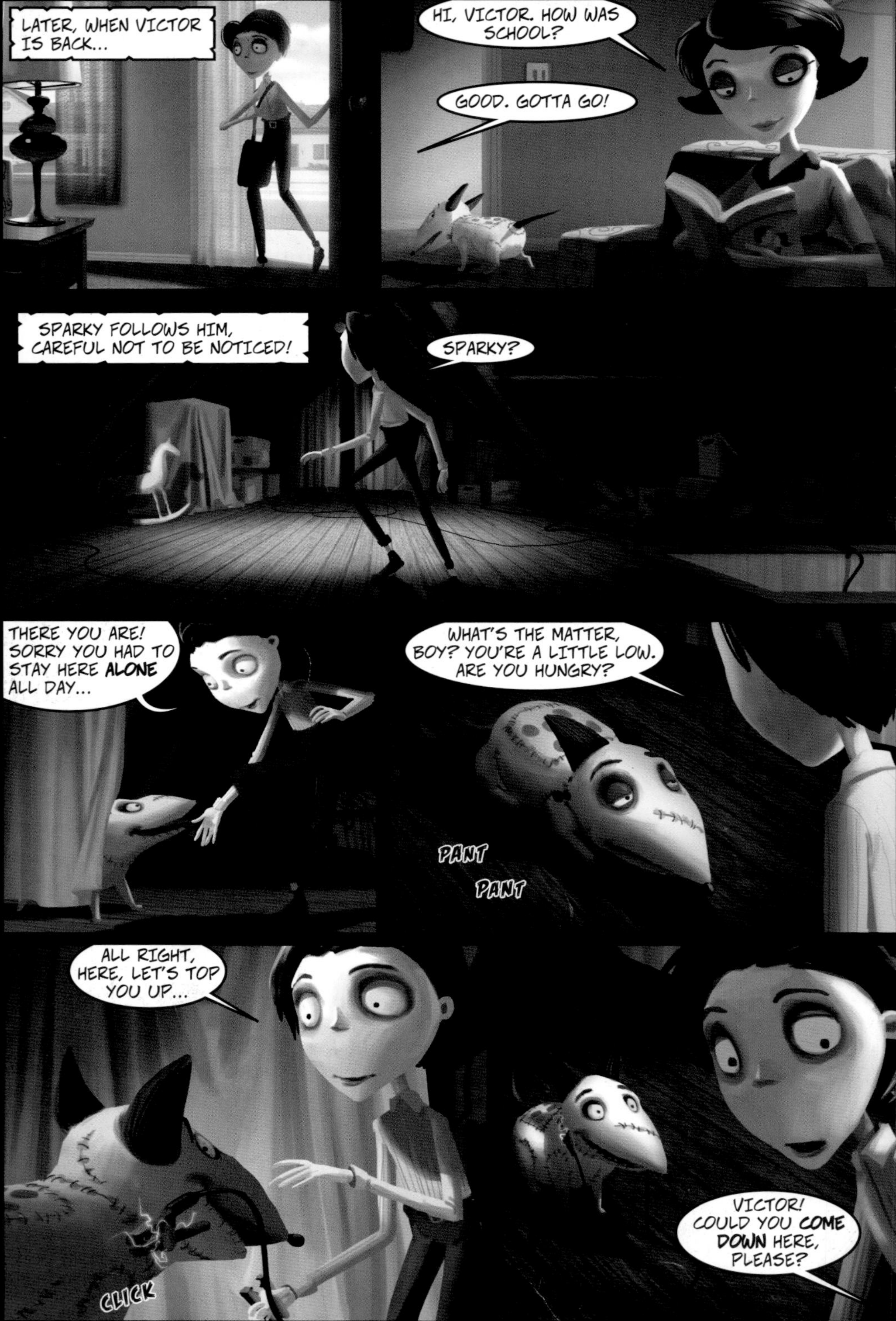
LATER, WHEN VICTOR IS BACK...
HI, VICTOR. HOW WAS SCHOOL?
GOOD. GOTTA GO!
SPARKY FOLLOWS HIM, CAREFUL NOT TO BE NOTICED!
SPARKY?
THERE YOU ARE! SORRY YOU HAD TO STAY HERE **ALONE** ALL DAY...
WHAT'S THE MATTER, BOY? YOU'RE A LITTLE LOW. ARE YOU HUNGRY?
PANT
PANT
ALL RIGHT, HERE, LET'S TOP YOU UP...
CLICK
VICTOR! COULD YOU **COME DOWN** HERE, PLEASE?

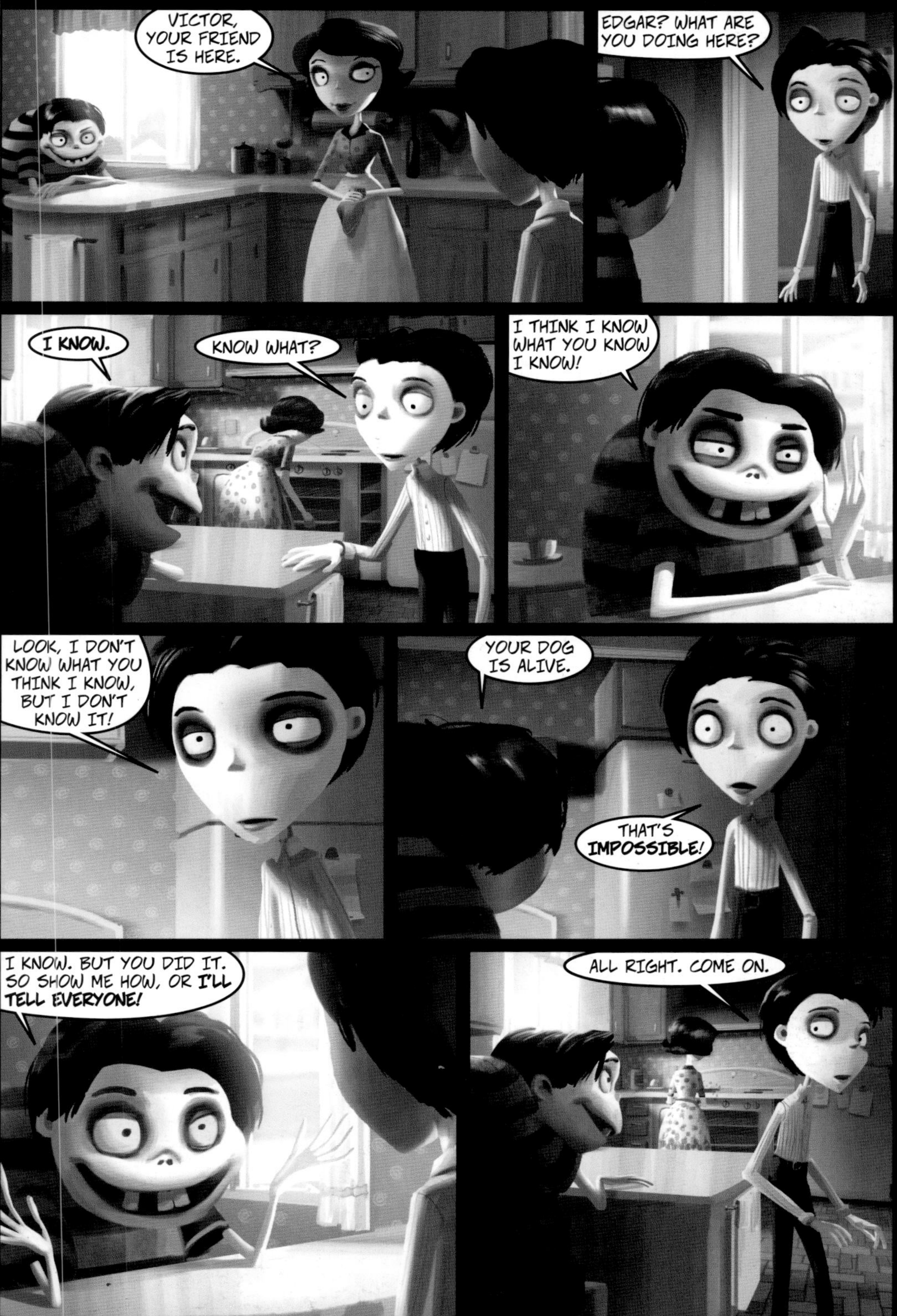
VICTOR, YOUR FRIEND IS HERE.
EDGAR? WHAT ARE YOU DOING HERE?
I KNOW.
KNOW WHAT?
I THINK I KNOW WHAT YOU KNOW I KNOW!
LOOK, I DON'T KNOW WHAT YOU THINK I KNOW, BUT I DON'T KNOW IT!
YOUR DOG IS ALIVE.
THAT'S IMPOSSIBLE!
I KNOW. BUT YOU DID IT. SO SHOW ME HOW, OR I'LL TELL EVERYONE!
ALL RIGHT. COME ON.

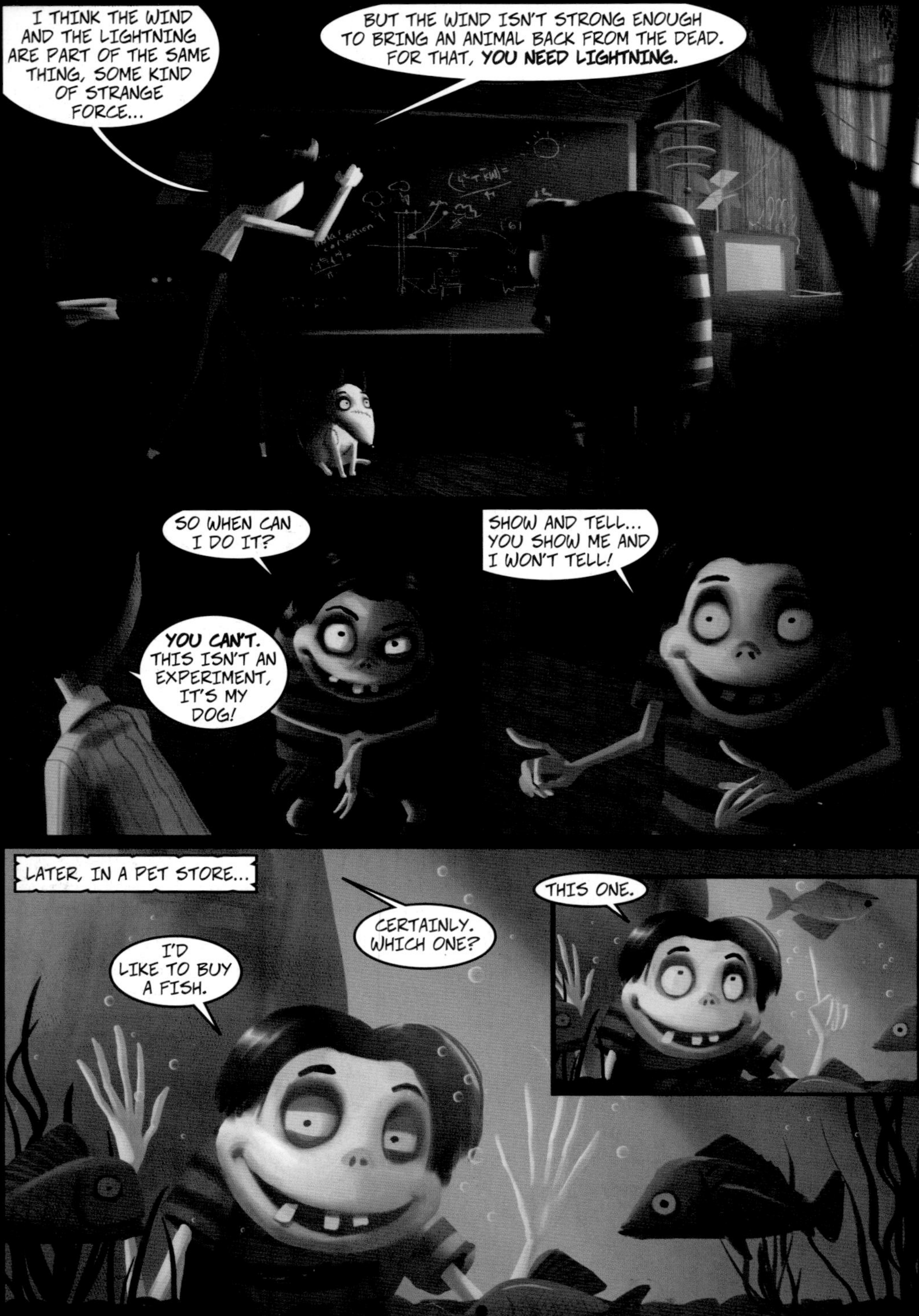
I THINK THE WIND AND THE LIGHTNING ARE PART OF THE SAME THING, SOME KIND OF STRANGE FORCE...
BUT THE WIND ISN'T STRONG ENOUGH TO BRING AN ANIMAL BACK FROM THE DEAD. FOR THAT, **YOU NEED LIGHTNING.**
SO WHEN CAN I DO IT?
YOU CAN'T. THIS ISN'T AN EXPERIMENT, IT'S MY DOG!
SHOW AND TELL... YOU SHOW ME AND I WON'T TELL!
LATER, IN A PET STORE...
I'D LIKE TO BUY A FISH.
CERTAINLY. WHICH ONE?
THIS ONE.

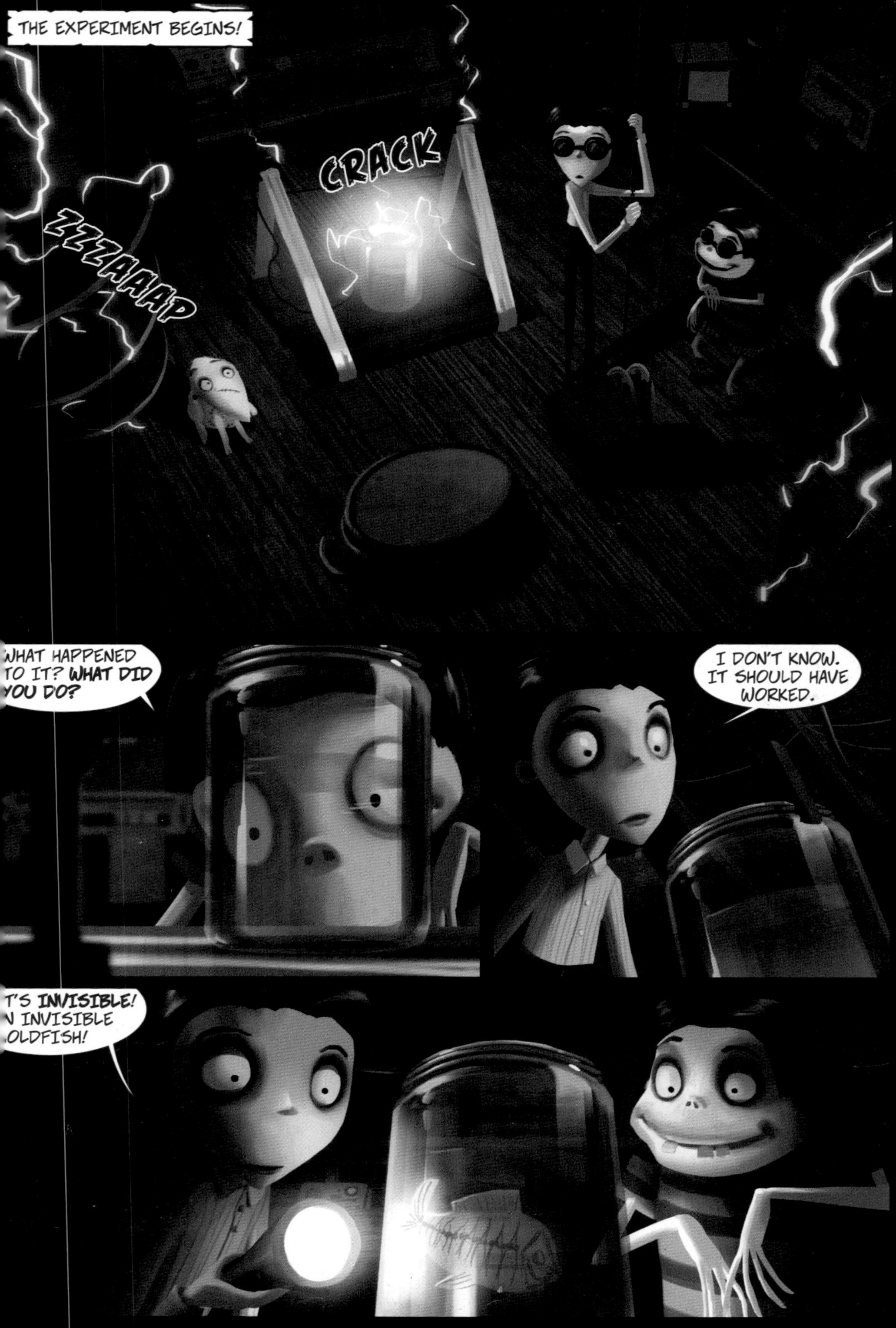
THE EXPERIMENT BEGINS!
CRACK
ZZZAAAAP
WHAT HAPPENED TO IT? WHAT DID YOU DO?
I DON'T KNOW. IT SHOULD HAVE WORKED.
T'S INVISIBLE! N INVISIBLE OLDFISH!

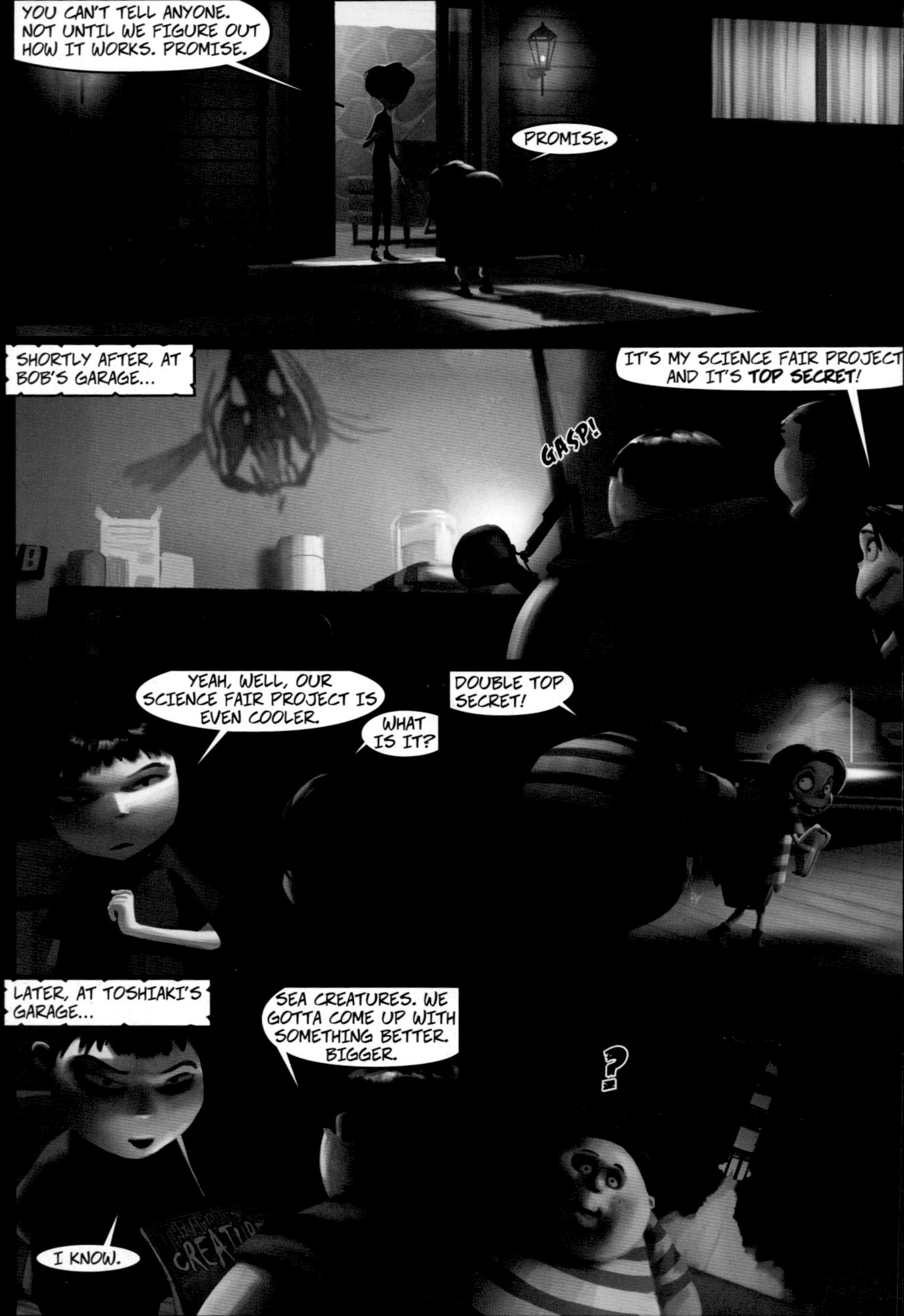
YOU CAN'T TELL ANYONE. NOT UNTIL WE FIGURE OUT HOW IT WORKS. PROMISE.
PROMISE.
SHORTLY AFTER, AT BOB'S GARAGE...
GASP!
IT'S MY SCIENCE FAIR PROJECT AND IT'S **TOP SECRET**!
YEAH, WELL, OUR SCIENCE FAIR PROJECT IS EVEN COOLER.
WHAT IS IT?
DOUBLE TOP SECRET!
LATER, AT TOSHIAKI'S GARAGE...
SEA CREATURES. WE GOTTA COME UP WITH SOMETHING BETTER. BIGGER.
?
I KNOW.

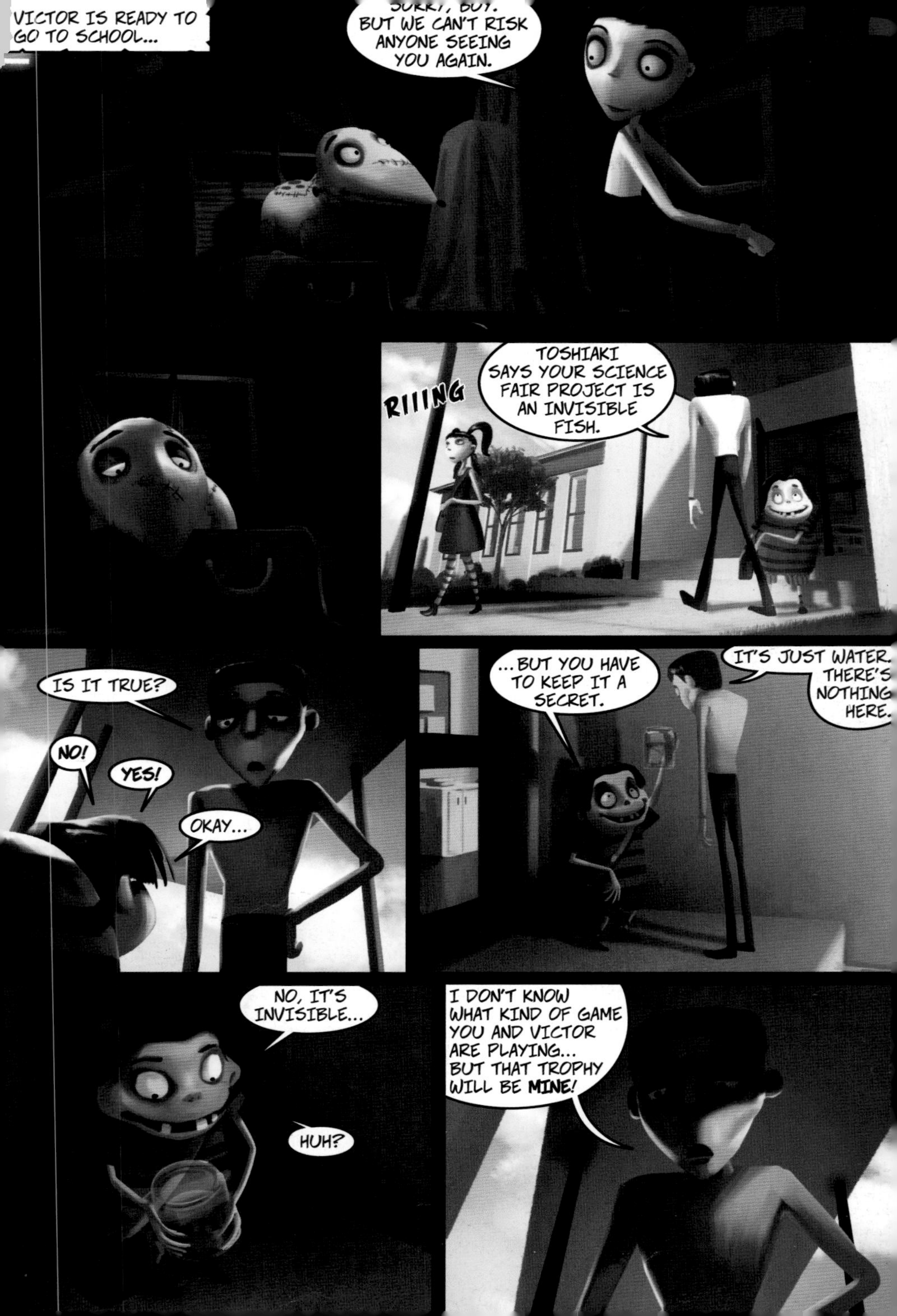

VICTOR IS READY TO GO TO SCHOOL...
BUT WE CAN'T RISK ANYONE SEEING YOU AGAIN.
RIIING
TOSHIAKI SAYS YOUR SCIENCE FAIR PROJECT IS AN INVISIBLE FISH.
IS IT TRUE?
NO!
YES!
OKAY...
...BUT YOU HAVE TO KEEP IT A SECRET.
IT'S JUST WATER. THERE'S NOTHING HERE.
NO, IT'S INVISIBLE...
HUH?
I DON'T KNOW WHAT KIND OF GAME YOU AND VICTOR ARE PLAYING... BUT THAT TROPHY WILL BE **MINE**!

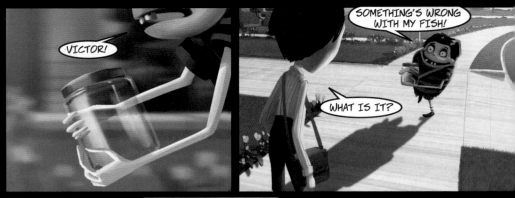

VICTOR!

SOMETHING'S WRONG WITH MY FISH!

WHAT IS IT?

IT'S NOT THERE ANYMORE!

MAYBE THEY DON'T LAST, MAYBE THEY'RE THERE FOR A LITTLE BIT...

?!

SPARKY!

LUCKILY...

DON'T WORRY. I CAN FIX THAT TOO...

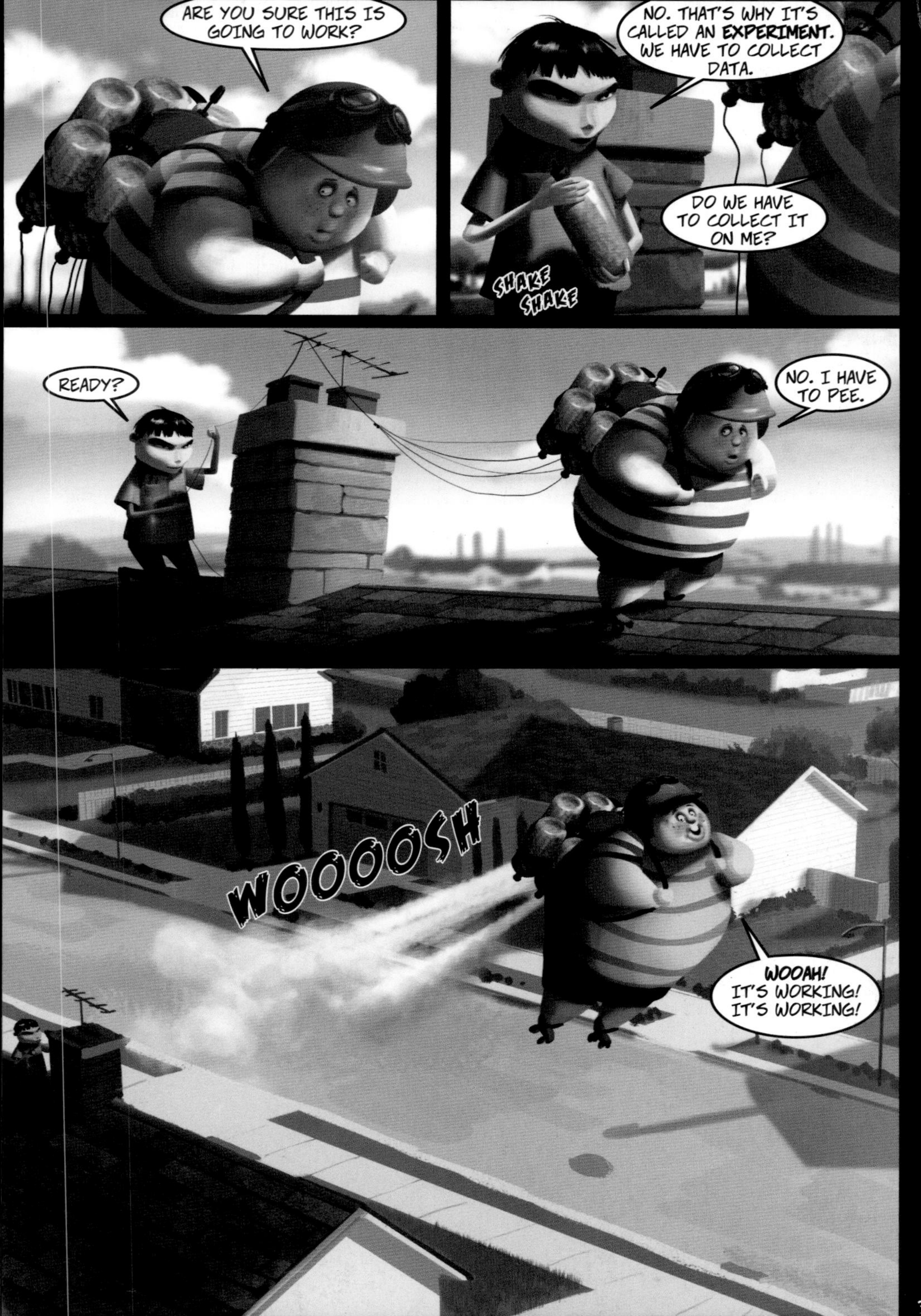
ARE YOU SURE THIS IS GOING TO WORK?
NO. THAT'S WHY IT'S CALLED AN **EXPERIMENT**. WE HAVE TO COLLECT DATA.
DO WE HAVE TO COLLECT IT ON ME?
SHAKE SHAKE
READY?
NO. I HAVE TO PEE.
WOOOOSH
WOOAH! IT'S WORKING! IT'S WORKING!

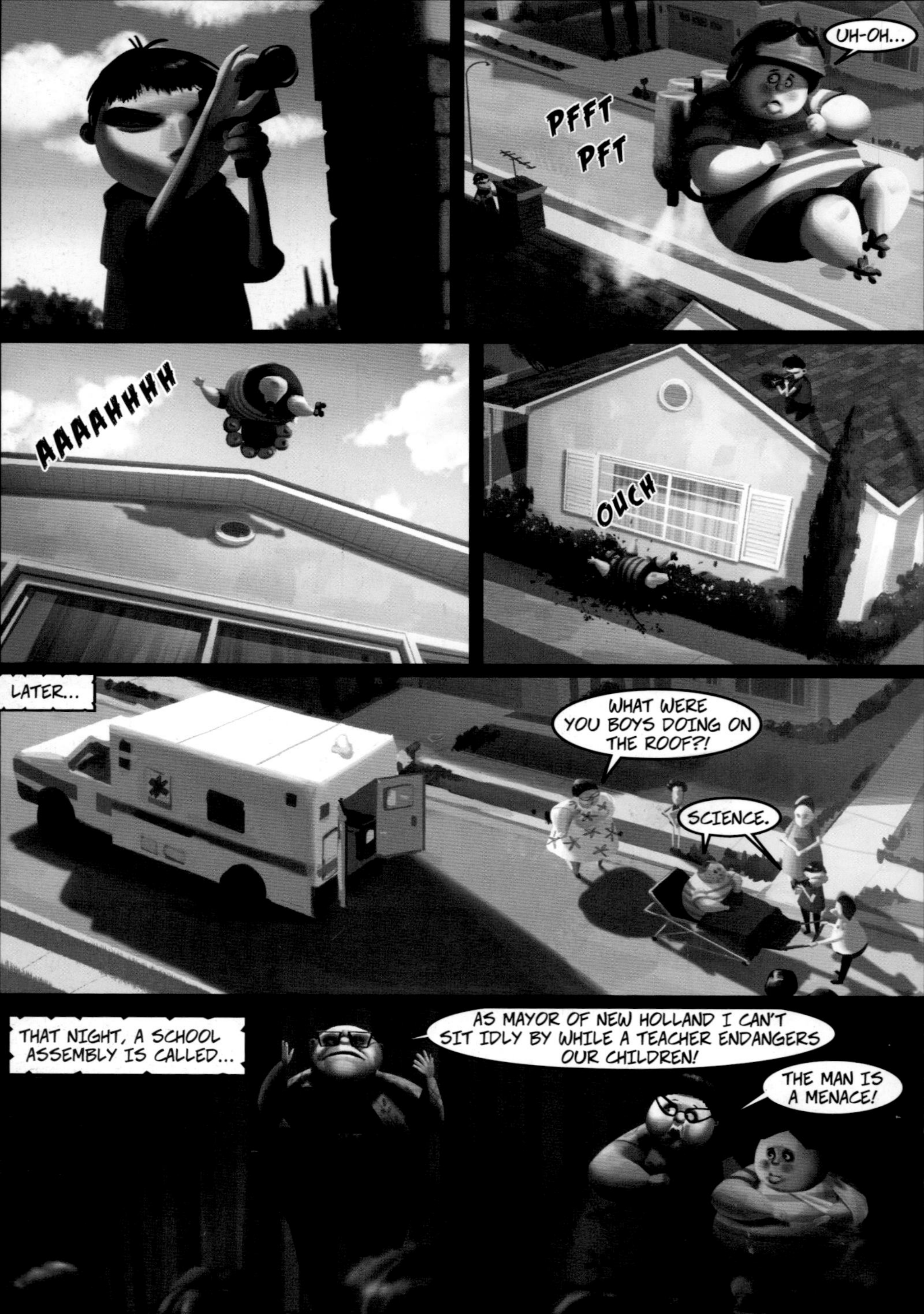
UH-OH...
PFFT
PFT
AAAAHHHH
OUCH
LATER...
WHAT WERE YOU BOYS DOING ON THE ROOF?!
SCIENCE.
THAT NIGHT, A SCHOOL ASSEMBLY IS CALLED...
AS MAYOR OF NEW HOLLAND I CAN'T SIT IDLY BY WHILE A TEACHER ENDANGERS OUR CHILDREN!
THE MAN IS A MENACE!

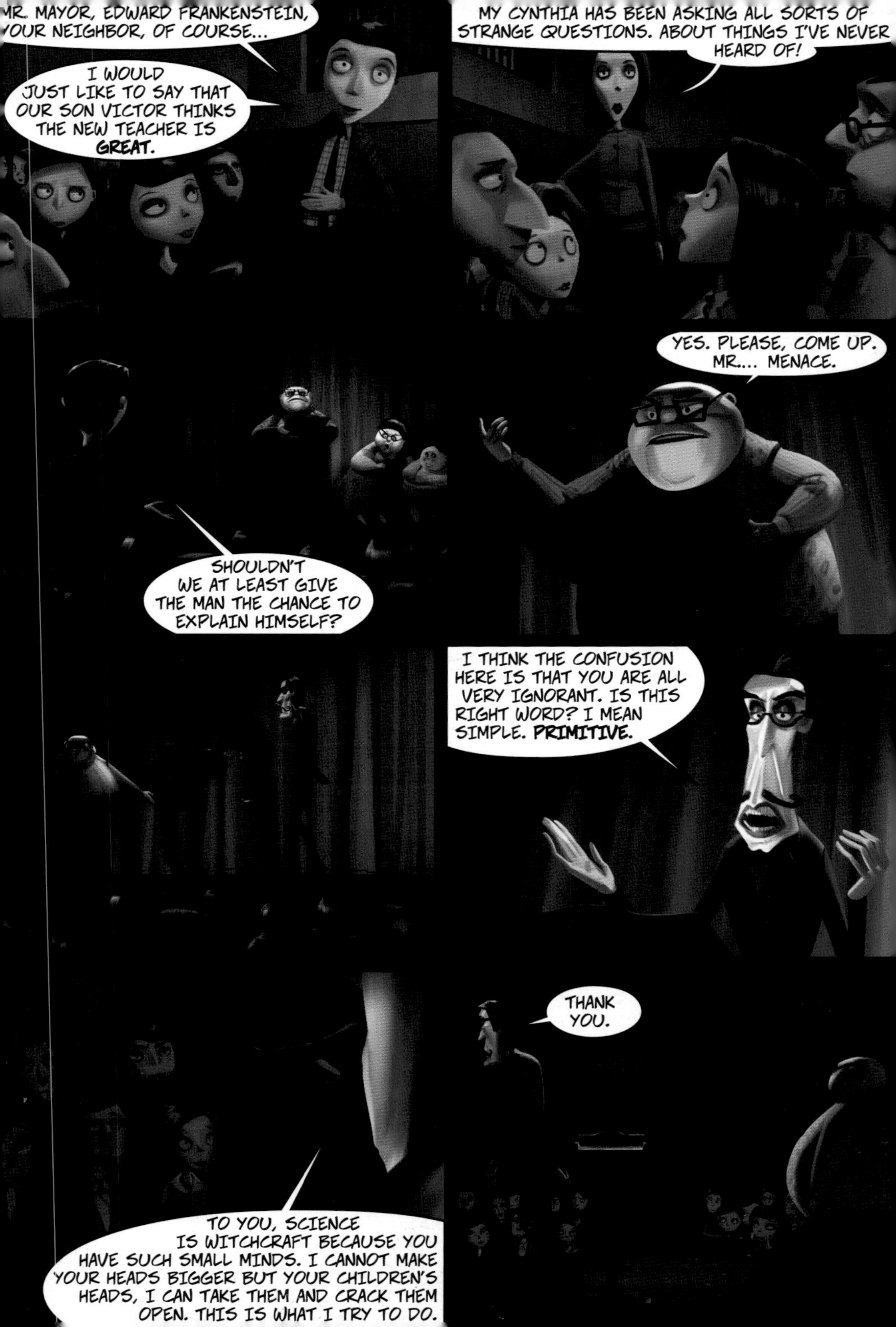
MR. MAYOR, EDWARD FRANKENSTEIN, YOUR NEIGHBOR, OF COURSE...
I WOULD JUST LIKE TO SAY THAT OUR SON VICTOR THINKS THE NEW TEACHER IS **GREAT**.
MY CYNTHIA HAS BEEN ASKING ALL SORTS OF STRANGE QUESTIONS. ABOUT THINGS I'VE NEVER HEARD OF!
SHOULDN'T WE AT LEAST GIVE THE MAN THE CHANCE TO EXPLAIN HIMSELF?
YES. PLEASE, COME UP. MR.... MENACE.
I THINK THE CONFUSION HERE IS THAT YOU ARE ALL VERY IGNORANT. IS THIS RIGHT WORD? I MEAN SIMPLE. **PRIMITIVE**.
TO YOU, SCIENCE IS WITCHCRAFT BECAUSE YOU HAVE SUCH SMALL MINDS. I CANNOT MAKE YOUR HEADS BIGGER BUT YOUR CHILDREN'S HEADS, I CAN TAKE THEM AND CRACK THEM OPEN. THIS IS WHAT I TRY TO DO.
THANK YOU.

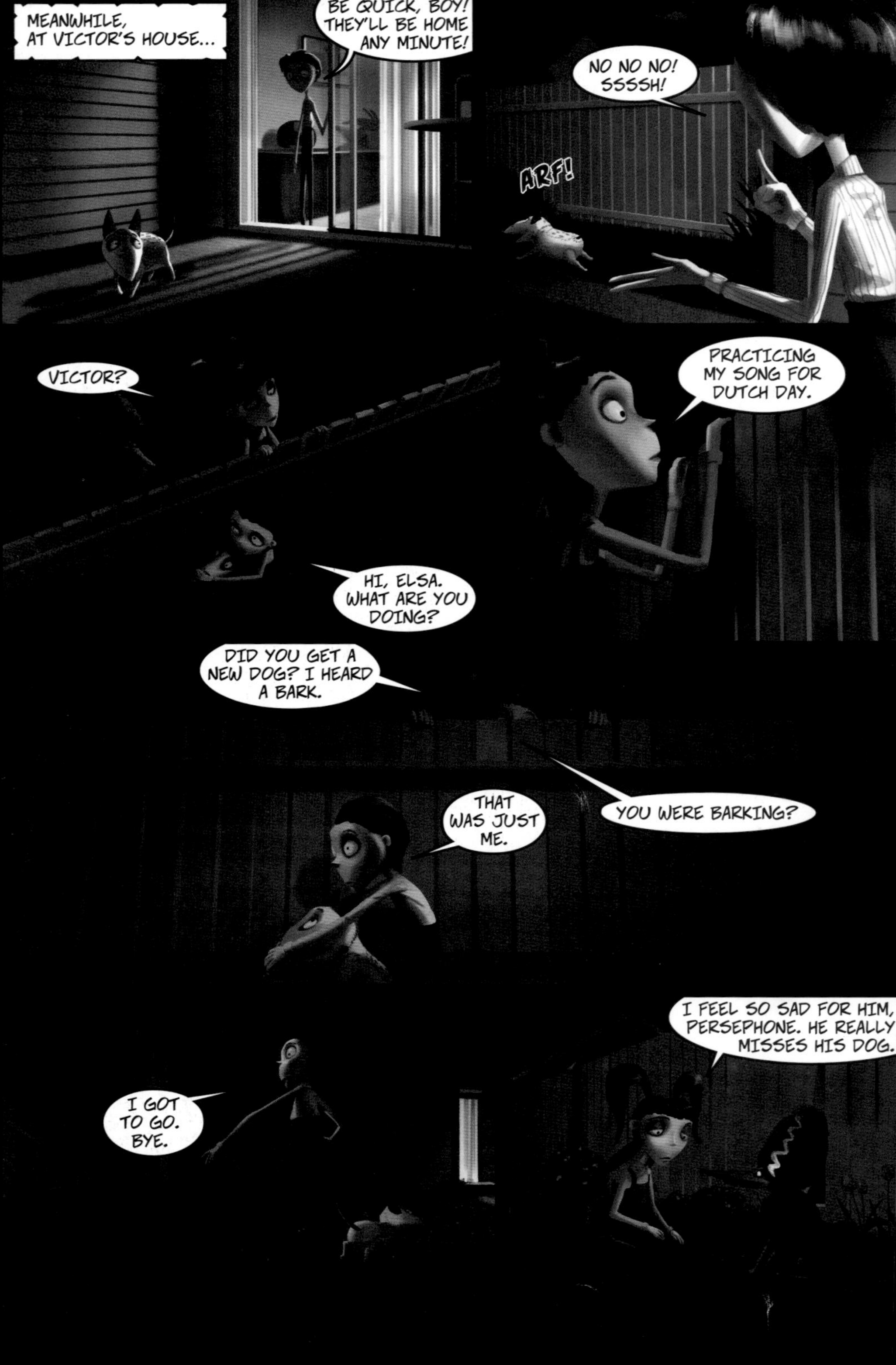
MEANWHILE, AT VICTOR'S HOUSE...
BE QUICK, BOY! THEY'LL BE HOME ANY MINUTE!
NO NO NO! SSSSH!
ARF!
VICTOR?
HI, ELSA. WHAT ARE YOU DOING?
PRACTICING MY SONG FOR DUTCH DAY.
DID YOU GET A NEW DOG? I HEARD A BARK.
THAT WAS JUST ME.
YOU WERE BARKING?
I GOT TO GO. BYE.
I FEEL SO SAD FOR HIM, PERSEPHONE. HE REALLY MISSES HIS DOG.

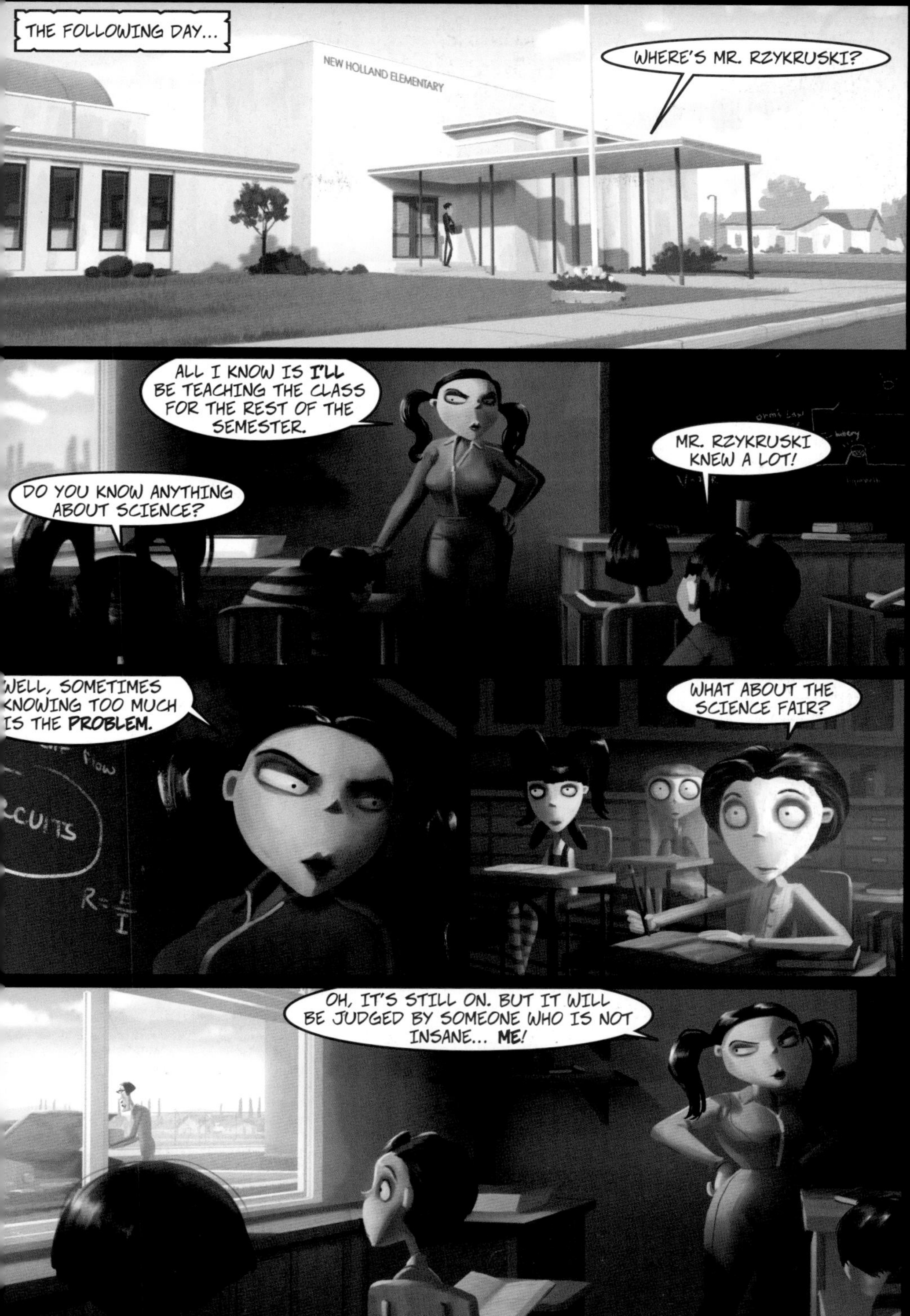
THE FOLLOWING DAY...
NEW HOLLAND ELEMENTARY
WHERE'S MR. RZYKRUSKI?
ALL I KNOW IS I'LL BE TEACHING THE CLASS FOR THE REST OF THE SEMESTER.
MR. RZYKRUSKI KNEW A LOT!
DO YOU KNOW ANYTHING ABOUT SCIENCE?
WELL, SOMETIMES KNOWING TOO MUCH IS THE PROBLEM.
WHAT ABOUT THE SCIENCE FAIR?
OH, IT'S STILL ON. BUT IT WILL BE JUDGED BY SOMEONE WHO IS NOT INSANE... ME!

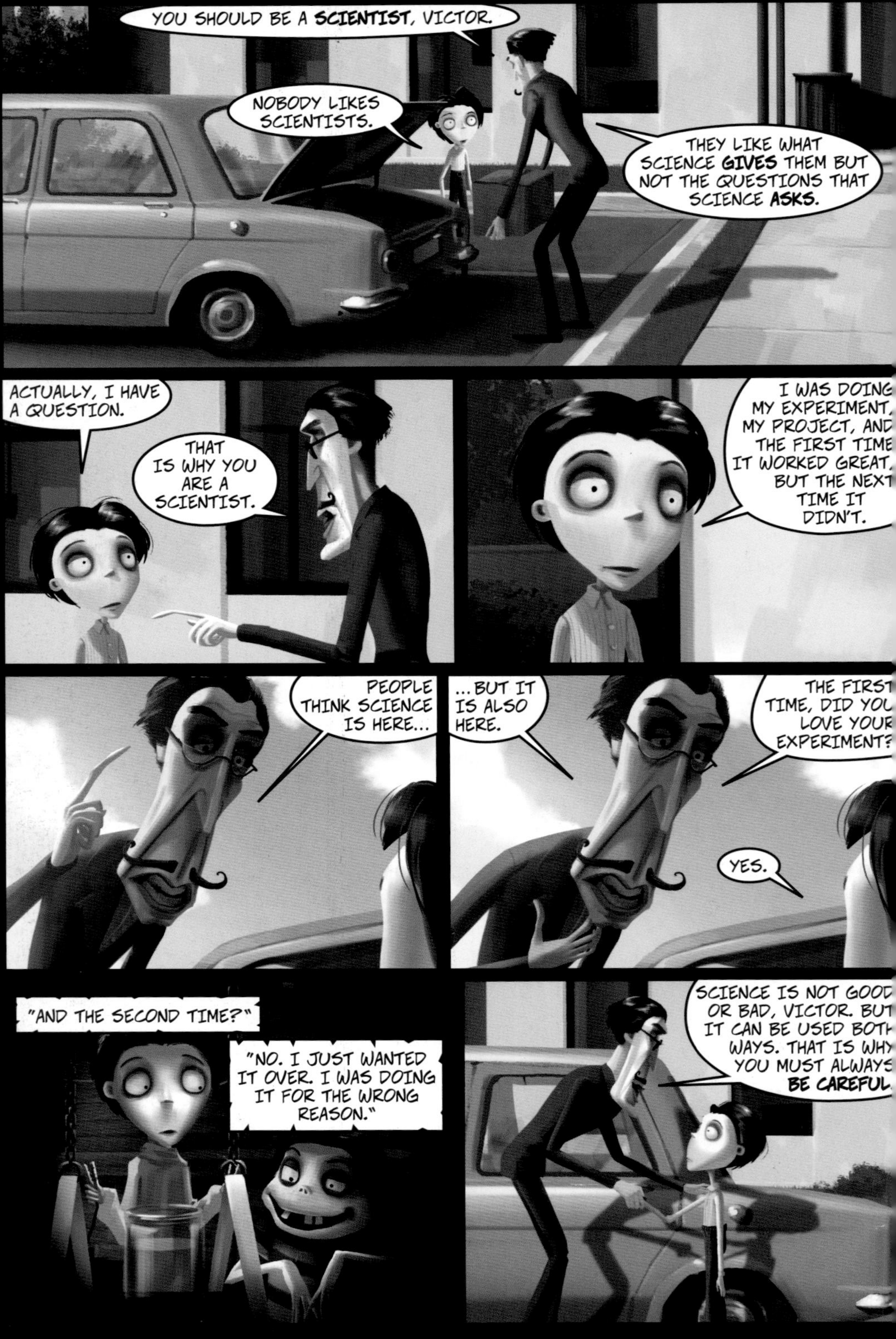
YOU SHOULD BE A **SCIENTIST**, VICTOR.
NOBODY LIKES SCIENTISTS.
THEY LIKE WHAT SCIENCE **GIVES** THEM BUT NOT THE QUESTIONS THAT SCIENCE **ASKS.**
ACTUALLY, I HAVE A QUESTION.
THAT IS WHY YOU ARE A SCIENTIST.
I WAS DOING MY EXPERIMENT, MY PROJECT, AND THE FIRST TIME IT WORKED GREAT, BUT THE NEXT TIME IT DIDN'T.
PEOPLE THINK SCIENCE IS HERE...
...BUT IT IS ALSO HERE.
THE FIRST TIME, DID YOU LOVE YOUR EXPERIMENT?
YES.
"AND THE SECOND TIME?"
"NO. I JUST WANTED IT OVER. I WAS DOING IT FOR THE WRONG REASON."
SCIENCE IS NOT GOOD OR BAD, VICTOR. BUT IT CAN BE USED BOTH WAYS. THAT IS WHY YOU MUST ALWAYS **BE CAREFUL.**

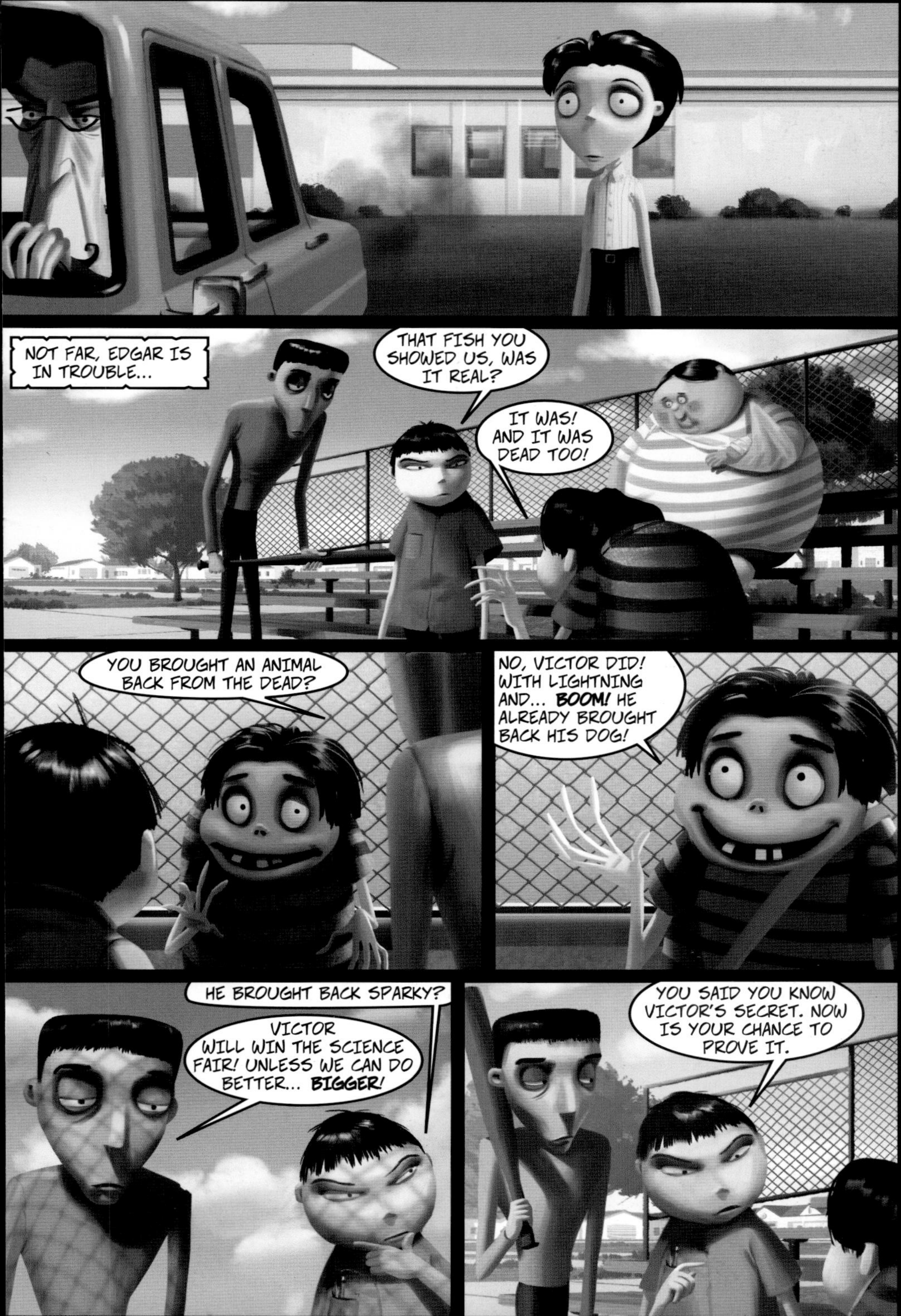
NOT FAR, EDGAR IS IN TROUBLE...
THAT FISH YOU SHOWED US, WAS IT REAL?
IT WAS! AND IT WAS DEAD TOO!
YOU BROUGHT AN ANIMAL BACK FROM THE DEAD?
NO, VICTOR DID! WITH LIGHTNING AND... **BOOM!** HE ALREADY BROUGHT BACK HIS DOG!
HE BROUGHT BACK SPARKY?
VICTOR WILL WIN THE SCIENCE FAIR! UNLESS WE CAN DO BETTER... **BIGGER**!
YOU SAID YOU KNOW VICTOR'S SECRET. NOW IS YOUR CHANCE TO PROVE IT.

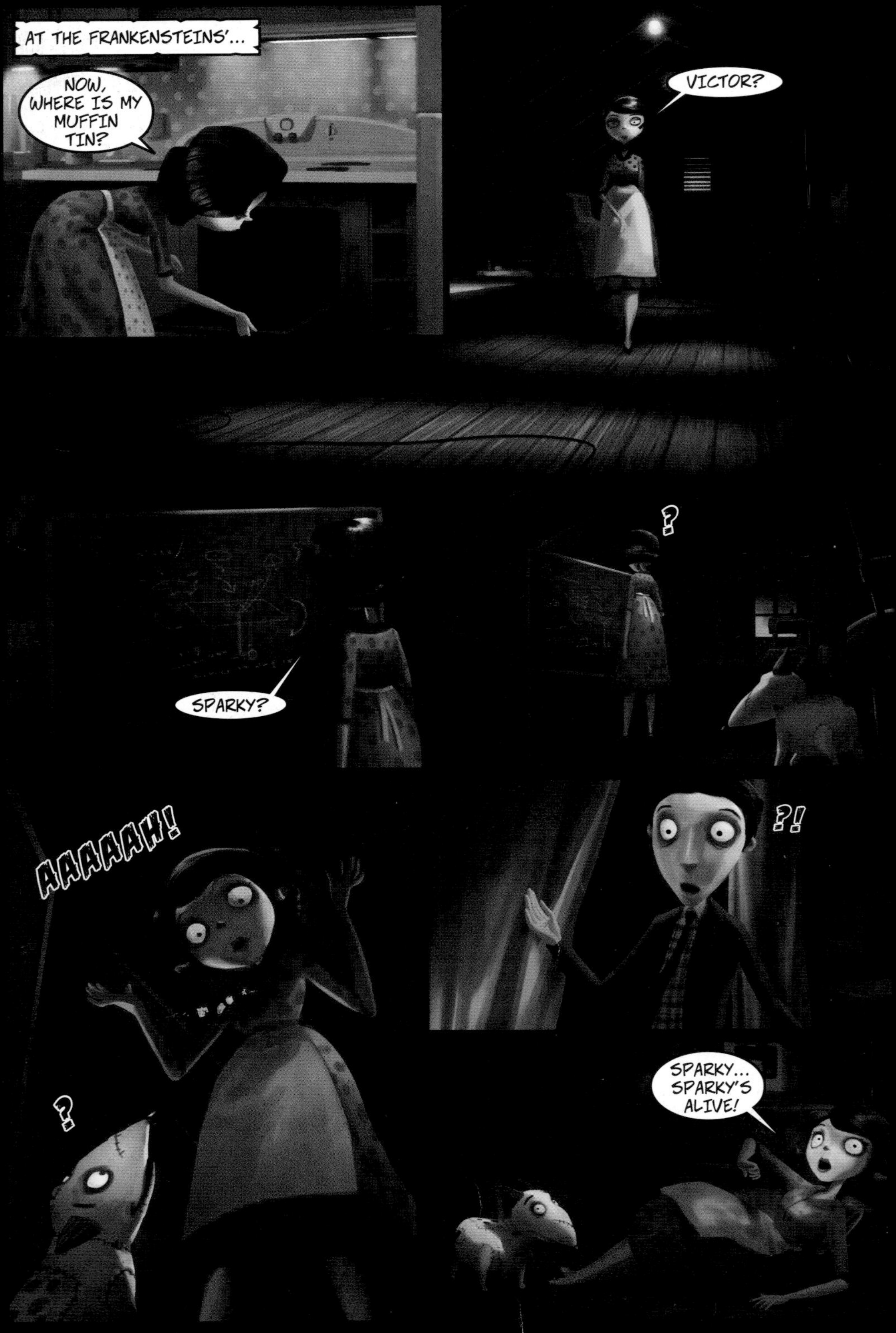
AT THE FRANKENSTEINS'...
NOW, WHERE IS MY MUFFIN TIN?
VICTOR?
SPARKY?
?
AAAAAAH!
?!
?
SPARKY... SPARKY'S ALIVE!

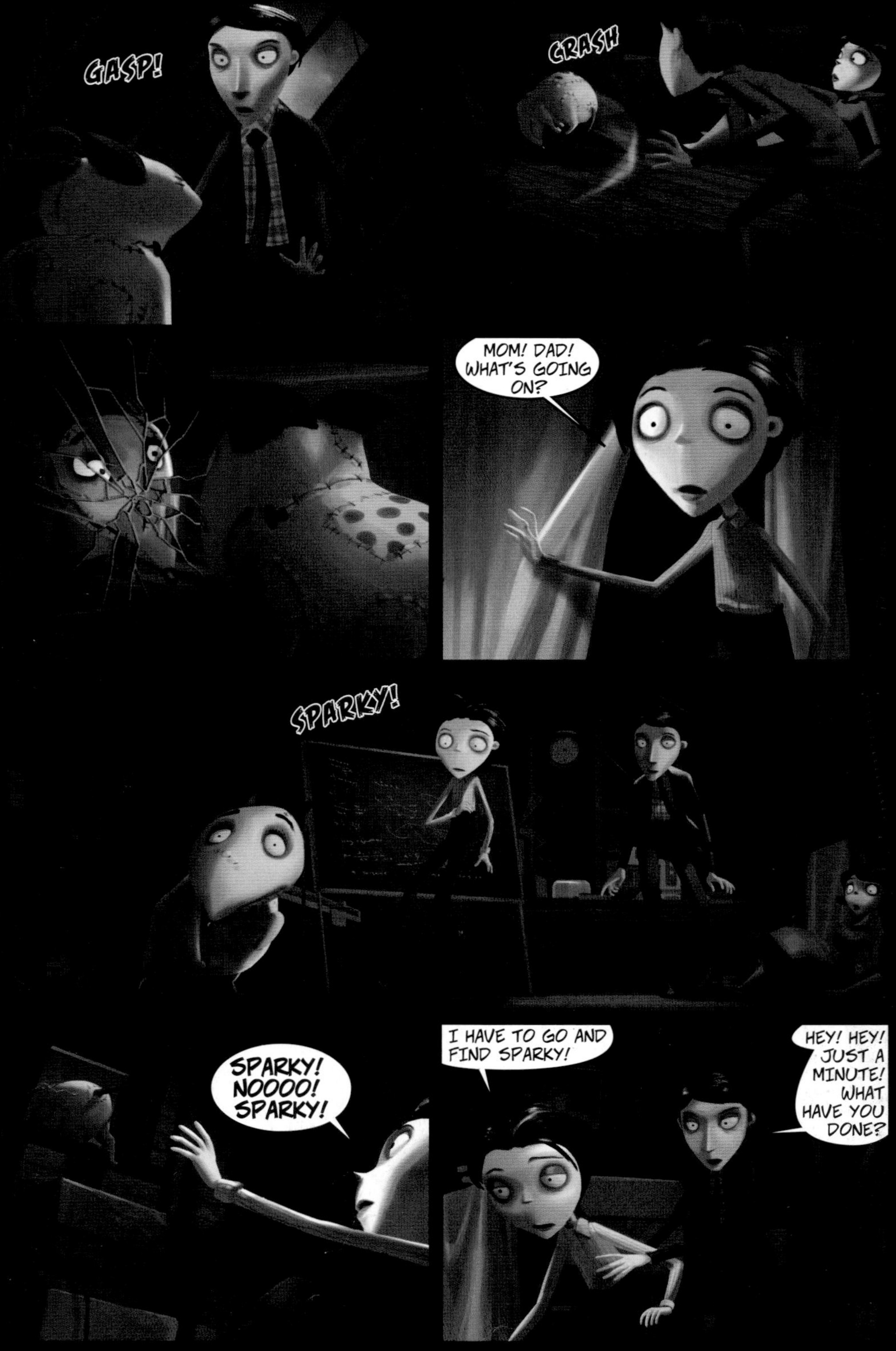
GASP!
CRASH
MOM! DAD! WHAT'S GOING ON?
SPARKY!
SPARKY! NOOOO! SPARKY!
I HAVE TO GO AND FIND SPARKY!
HEY! HEY! JUST A MINUTE! WHAT HAVE YOU DONE?

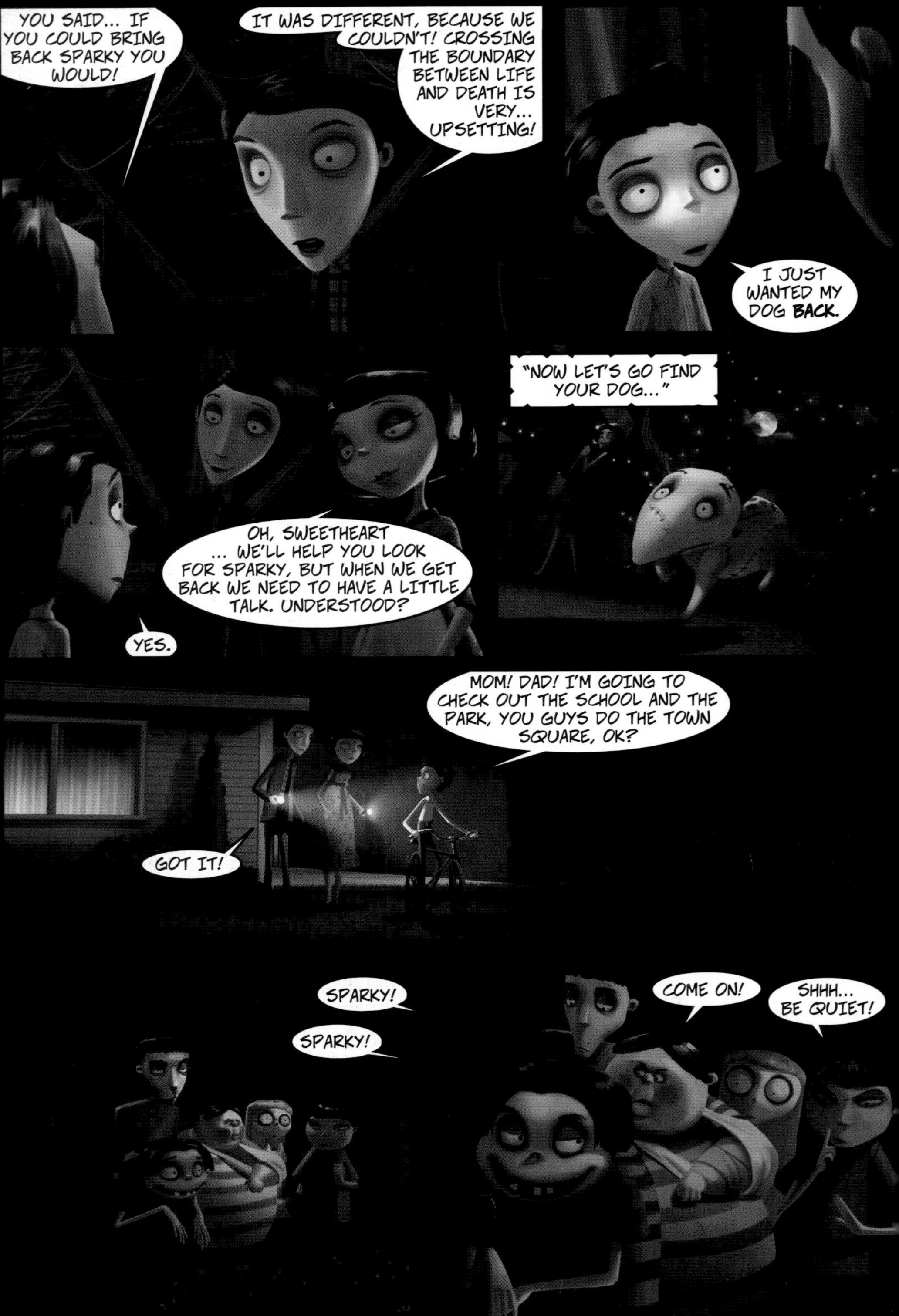
YOU SAID... IF YOU COULD BRING BACK SPARKY YOU WOULD!
IT WAS DIFFERENT, BECAUSE WE COULDN'T! CROSSING THE BOUNDARY BETWEEN LIFE AND DEATH IS VERY... UPSETTING!
I JUST WANTED MY DOG BACK.
OH, SWEETHEART ... WE'LL HELP YOU LOOK FOR SPARKY, BUT WHEN WE GET BACK WE NEED TO HAVE A LITTLE TALK. UNDERSTOOD?
YES.
"NOW LET'S GO FIND YOUR DOG..."
MOM! DAD! I'M GOING TO CHECK OUT THE SCHOOL AND THE PARK, YOU GUYS DO THE TOWN SQUARE, OK?
GOT IT!
SPARKY!
SPARKY!
COME ON!
SHHH... BE QUIET!

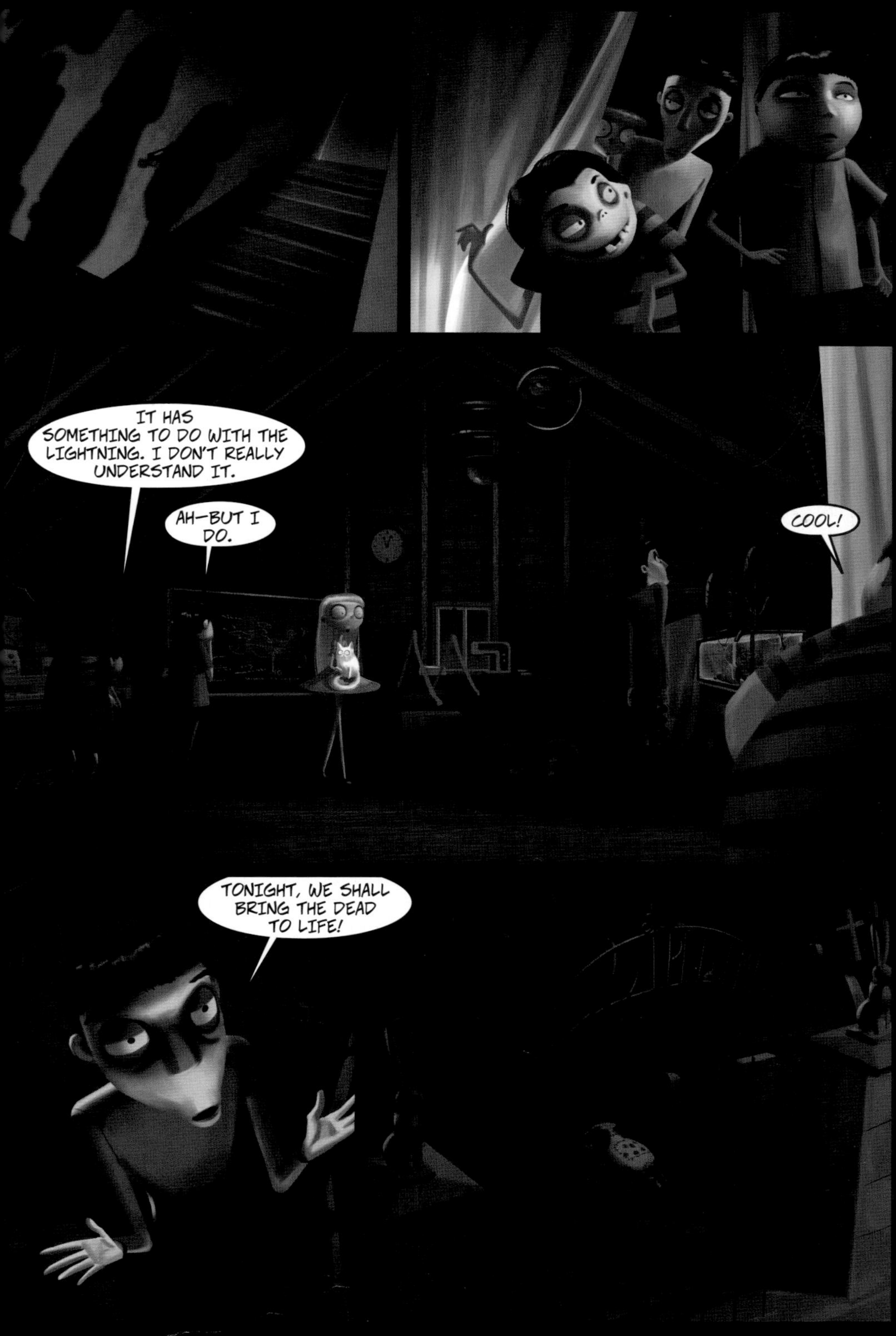
IT HAS SOMETHING TO DO WITH THE LIGHTNING. I DON'T REALLY UNDERSTAND IT.
AH—BUT I DO.
COOL!
TONIGHT, WE SHALL BRING THE DEAD TO LIFE!

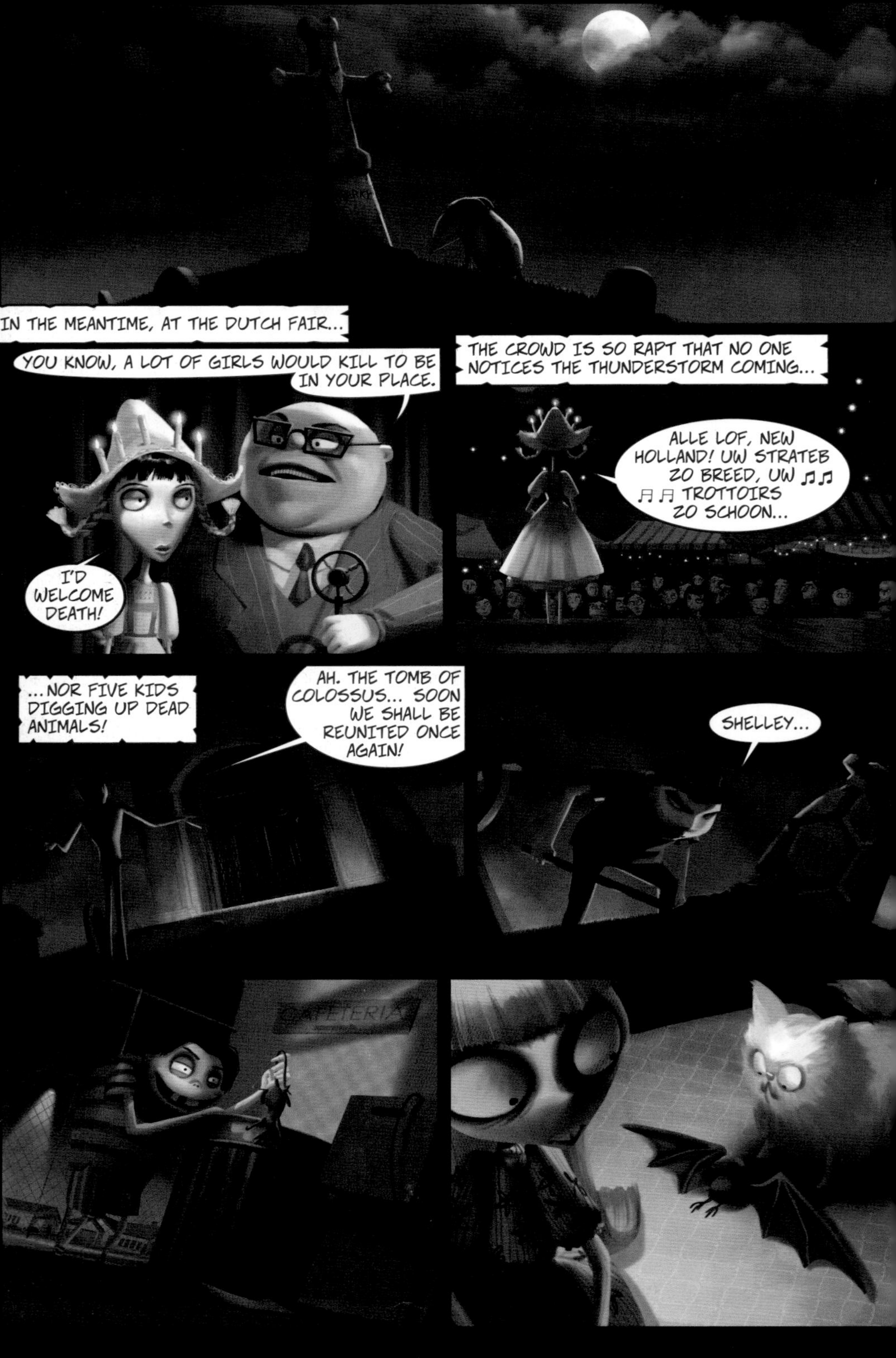

IN THE MEANTIME, AT THE DUTCH FAIR...
YOU KNOW, A LOT OF GIRLS WOULD KILL TO BE IN YOUR PLACE.
I'D WELCOME DEATH!
THE CROWD IS SO RAPT THAT NO ONE NOTICES THE THUNDERSTORM COMING...
ALLE LOF, NEW HOLLAND! UW STRATEB ZO BREED, UW ♫♫ ♫♫ TROTTOIRS ZO SCHOON...
...NOR FIVE KIDS DIGGING UP DEAD ANIMALS!
AH. THE TOMB OF COLOSSUS... SOON WE SHALL BE REUNITED ONCE AGAIN!
SHELLEY...

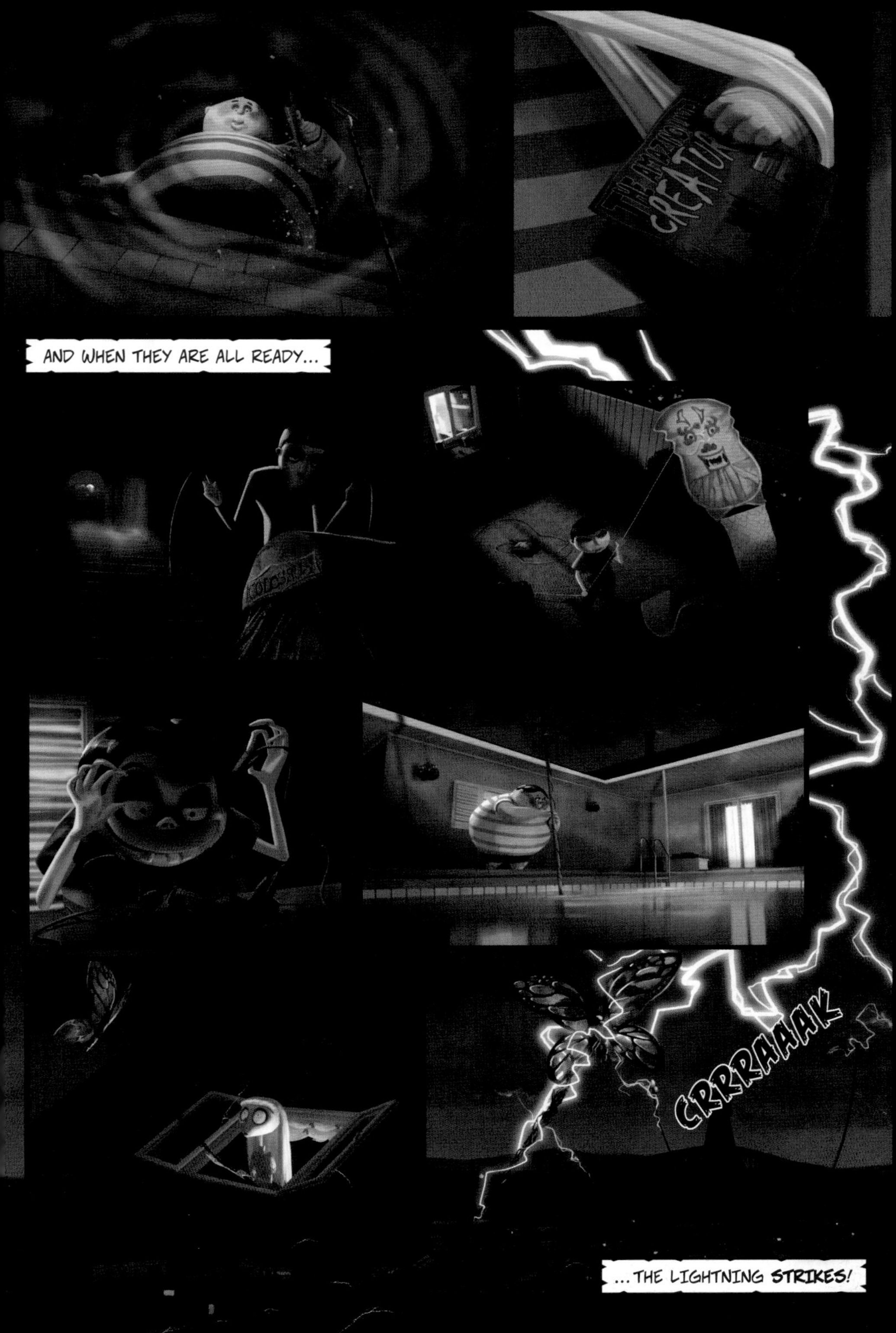
AND WHEN THEY ARE ALL READY...
CRRRAAAK
...THE LIGHTNING **STRIKES**!

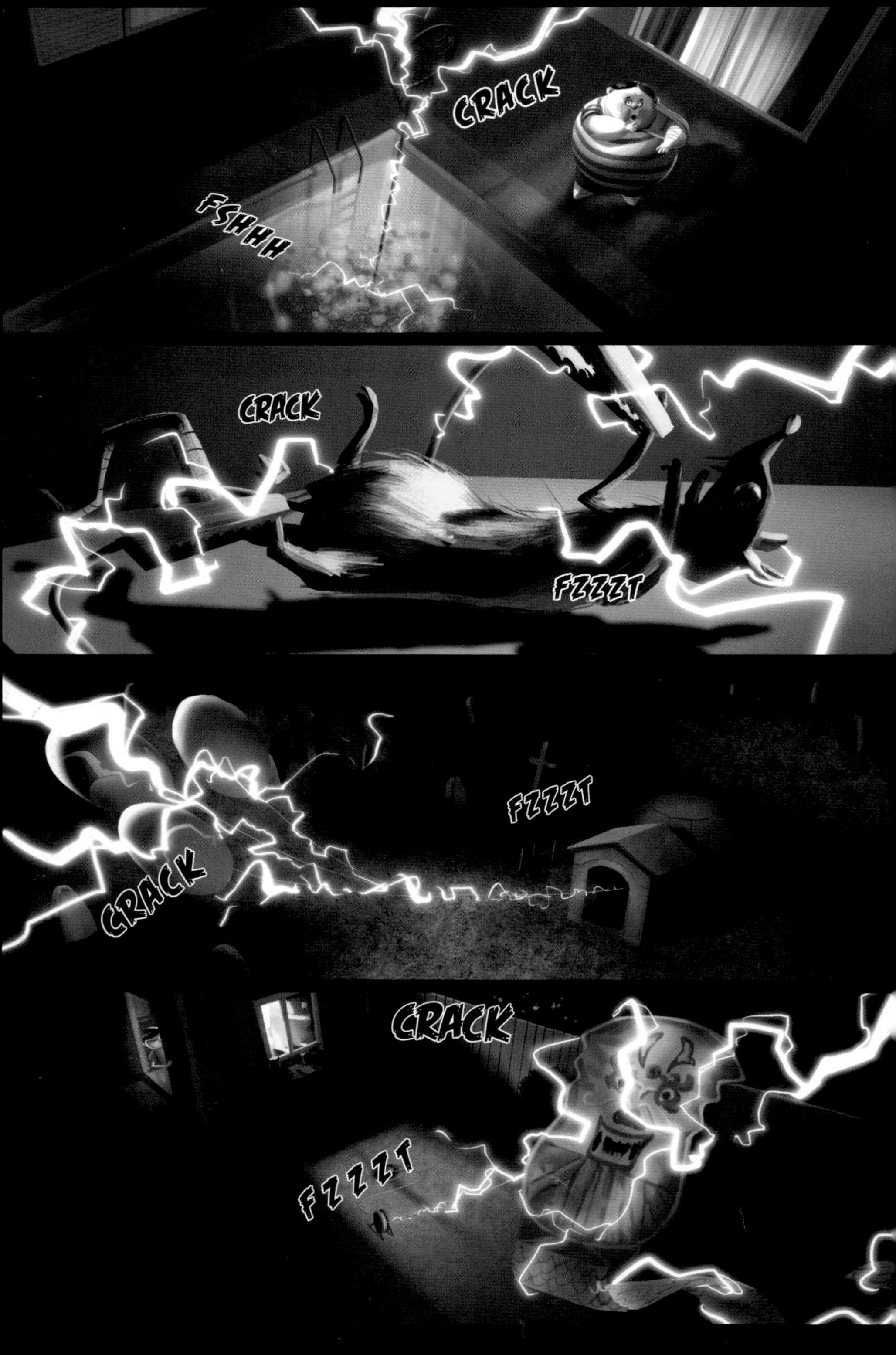
CRACK
FSHHH
CRACK
FZZZT
FZZZT
CRACK
CRACK
FZZZT

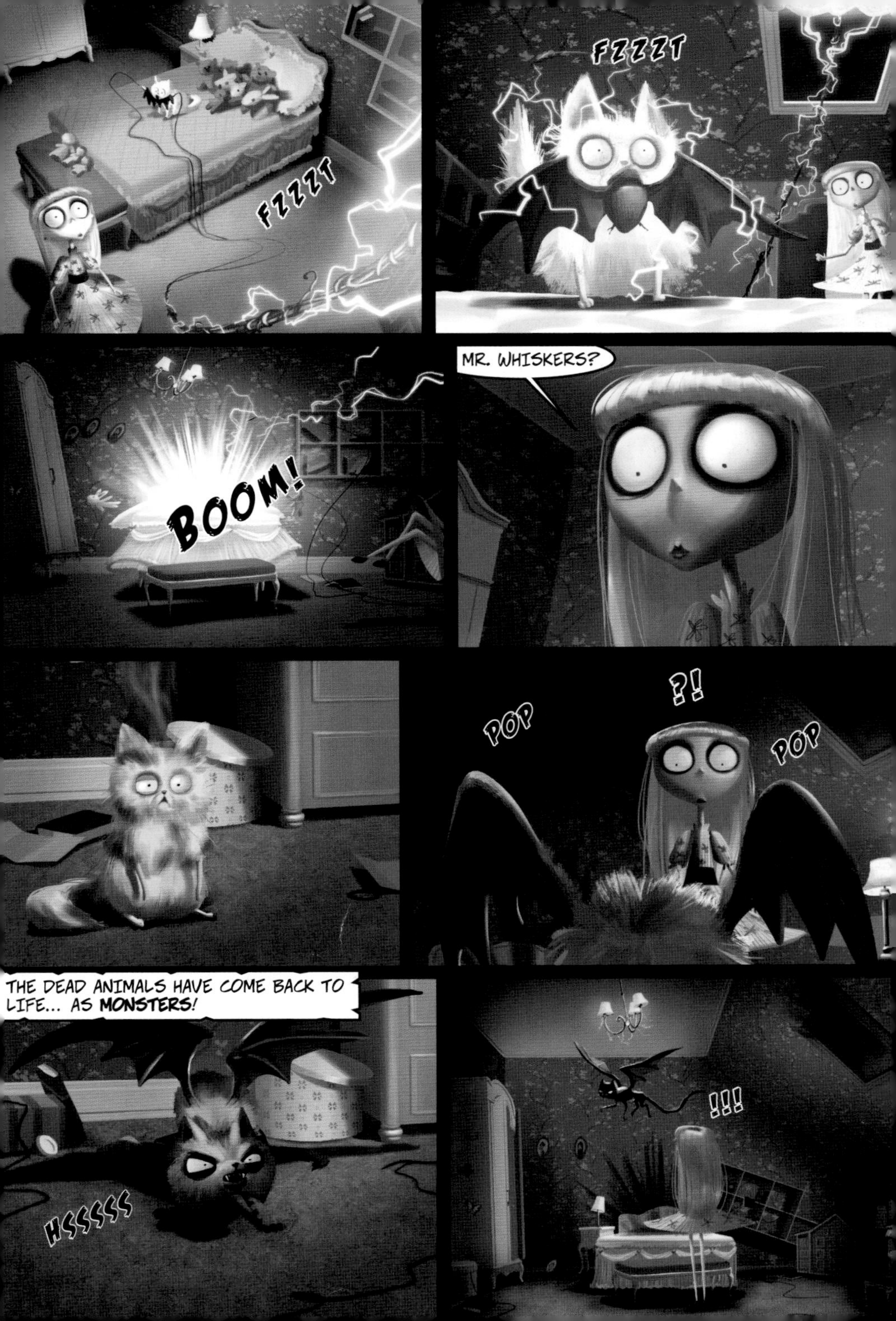
FZZZT
FZZZT
BOOM!
MR. WHISKERS?
?!
POP
POP
THE DEAD ANIMALS HAVE COME BACK TO LIFE... AS **MONSTERS**!
HSSSSS
!!!

VAMPIRE CAT!

AAAAAAH!

GRRRR

WERE-RAT!

RISE, COLOSSUS! RISE FROM YOUR TOMB!

WELL, JUST... MUMMY HAMSTER!

?!

GIANT MUMMY HAMSTER!
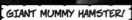

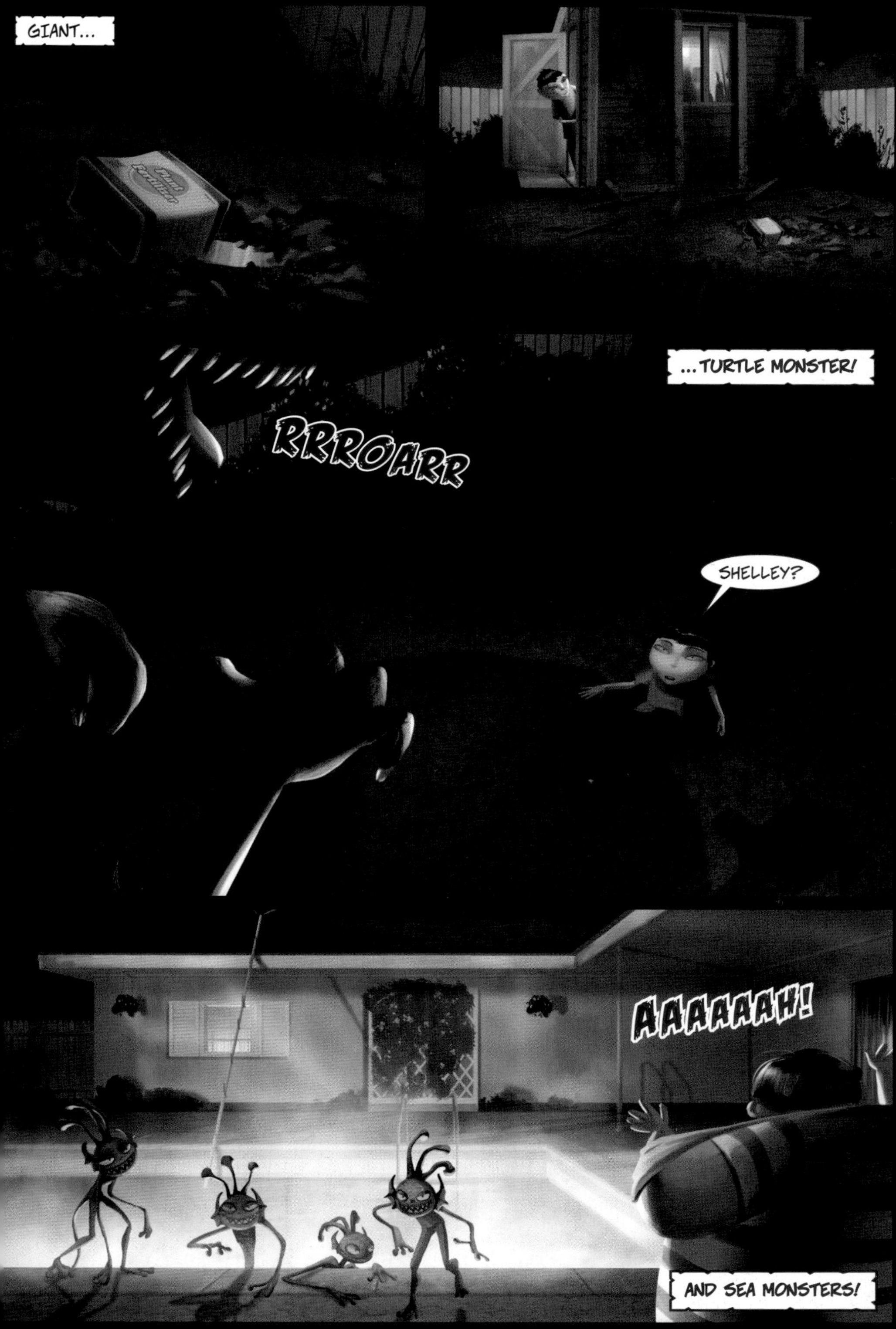
GIANT...
...TURTLE MONSTER!
RRROARR
SHELLEY?
AAAAAAH!
AND SEA MONSTERS!

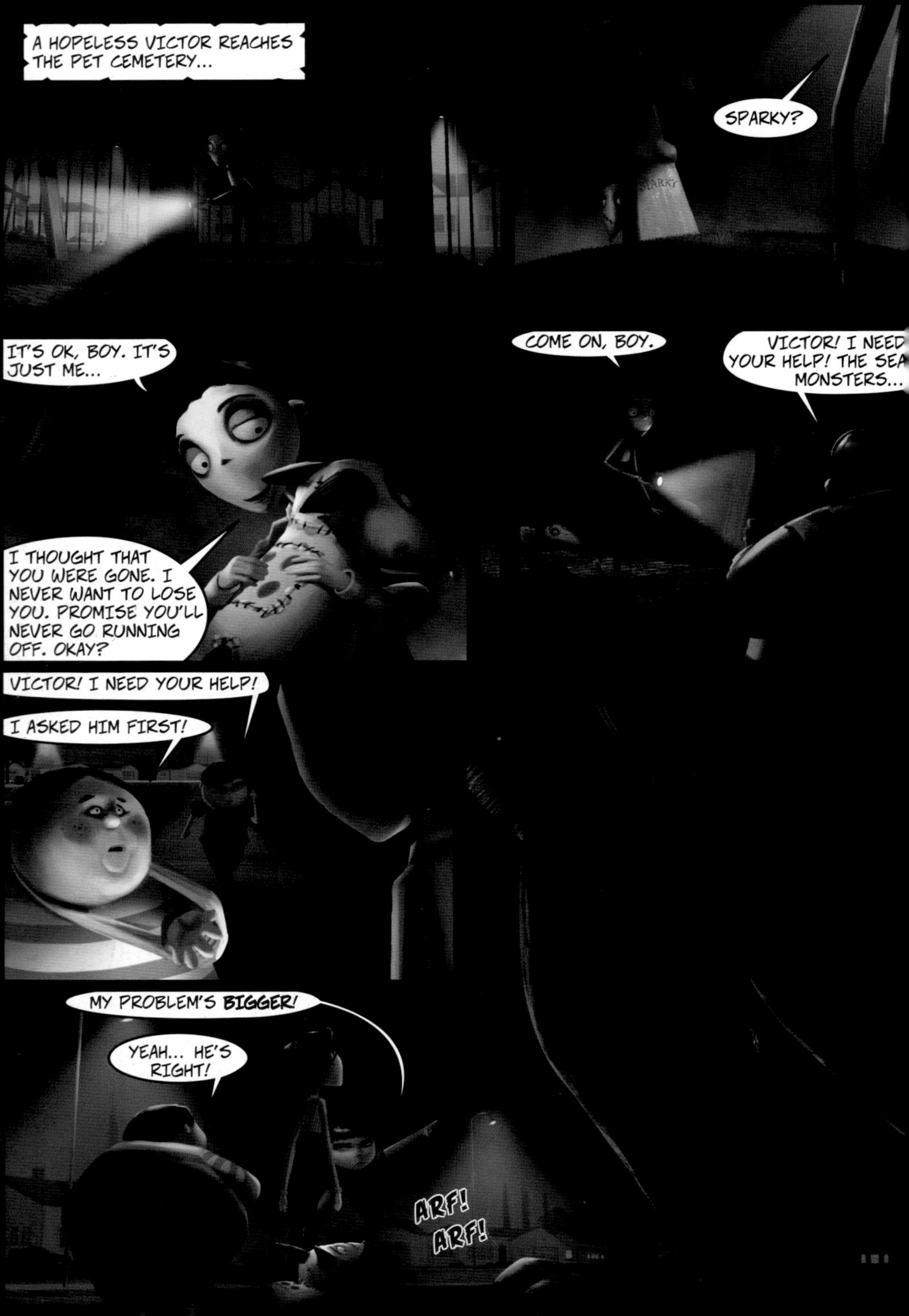
A HOPELESS VICTOR REACHES THE PET CEMETERY...
SPARKY?
SPARKY
IT'S OK, BOY. IT'S JUST ME...
I THOUGHT THAT YOU WERE GONE. I NEVER WANT TO LOSE YOU. PROMISE YOU'LL NEVER GO RUNNING OFF. OKAY?
COME ON, BOY.
VICTOR! I NEED YOUR HELP! THE SEA MONSTERS...
VICTOR! I NEED YOUR HELP!
I ASKED HIM FIRST!
MY PROBLEM'S **BIGGER**!
YEAH... HE'S RIGHT!
ARF! ARF!

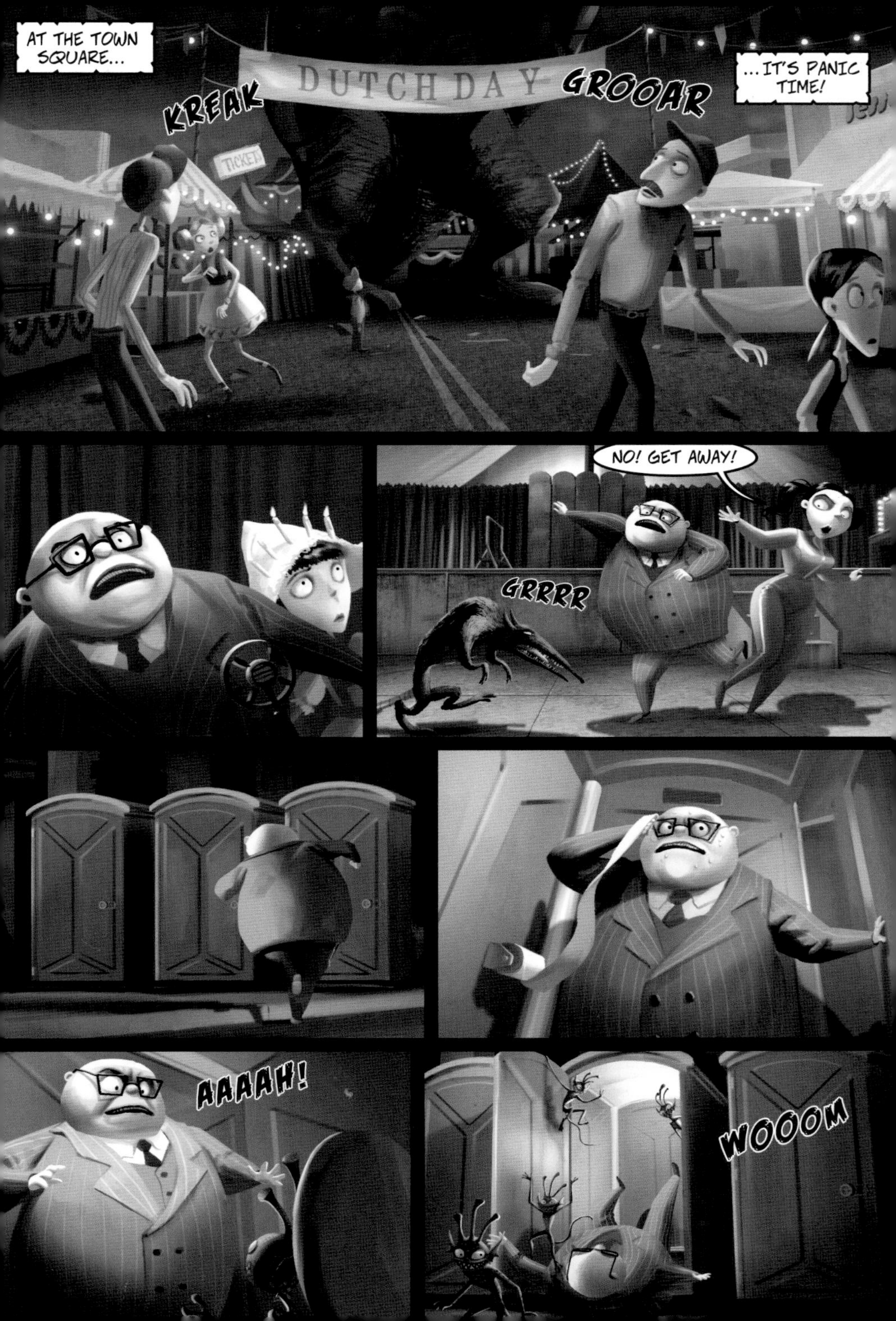
AT THE TOWN SQUARE...
DUTCH DAY
KREAK
GROOAR
...IT'S PANIC TIME!
TICKETS
NO! GET AWAY!
GRRRR
AAAAH!
WOOOM

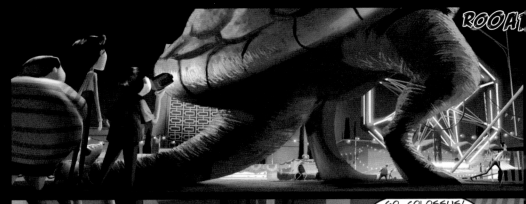

ROOA

GGRRR

GO, COLOSSUS! KILL! KILL! KILL!

GGRRR

SPLAT

RRROARR

AAAAAAH

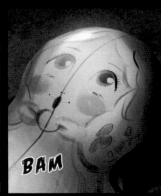

BAM

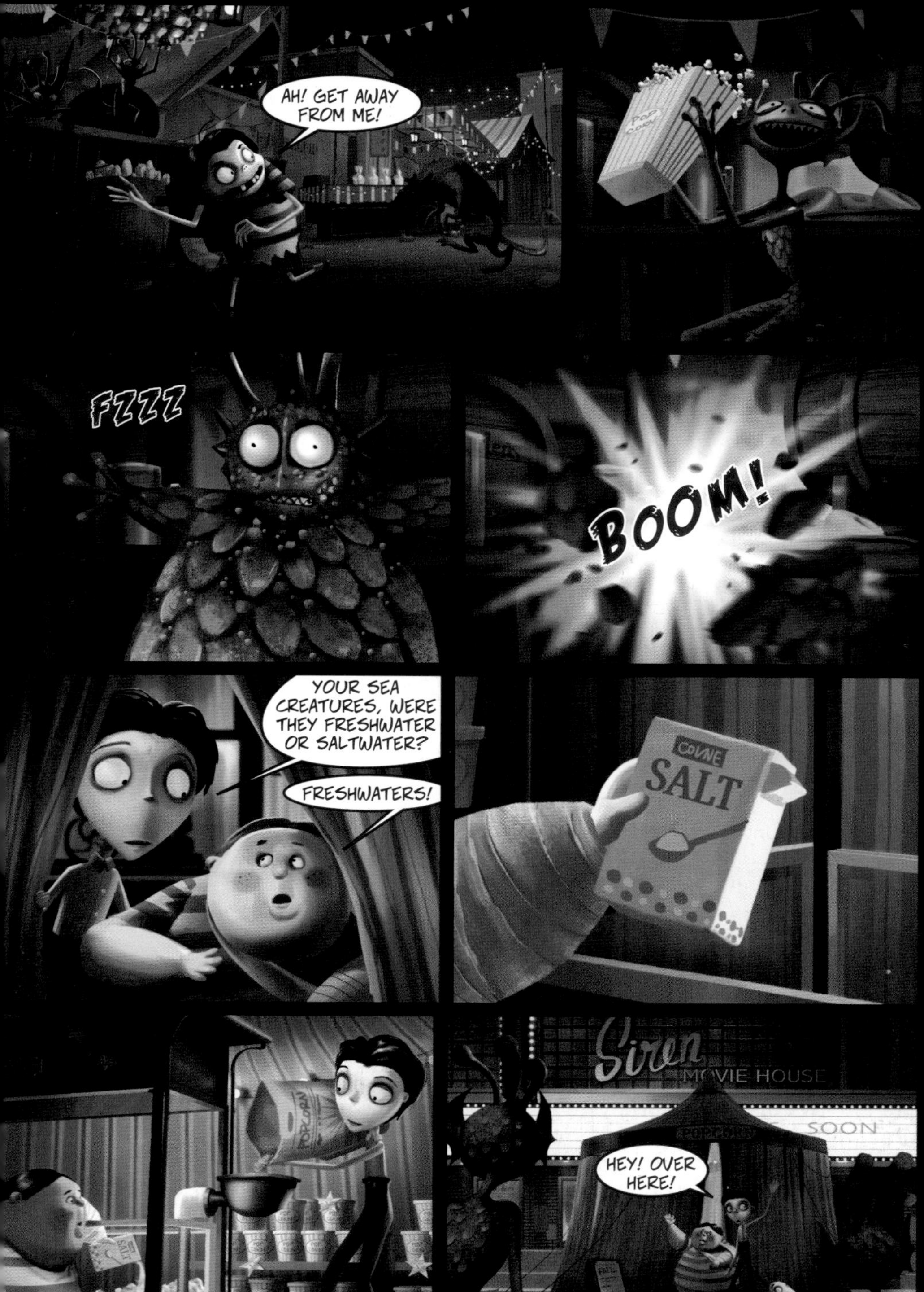
AH! GET AWAY FROM ME!
FZZZ
BOOM!
YOUR SEA CREATURES, WERE THEY FRESHWATER OR SALTWATER?
FRESHWATERS!
SALT
POPCORN
Siren
MOVIE HOUSE
SOON
HEY! OVER HERE!

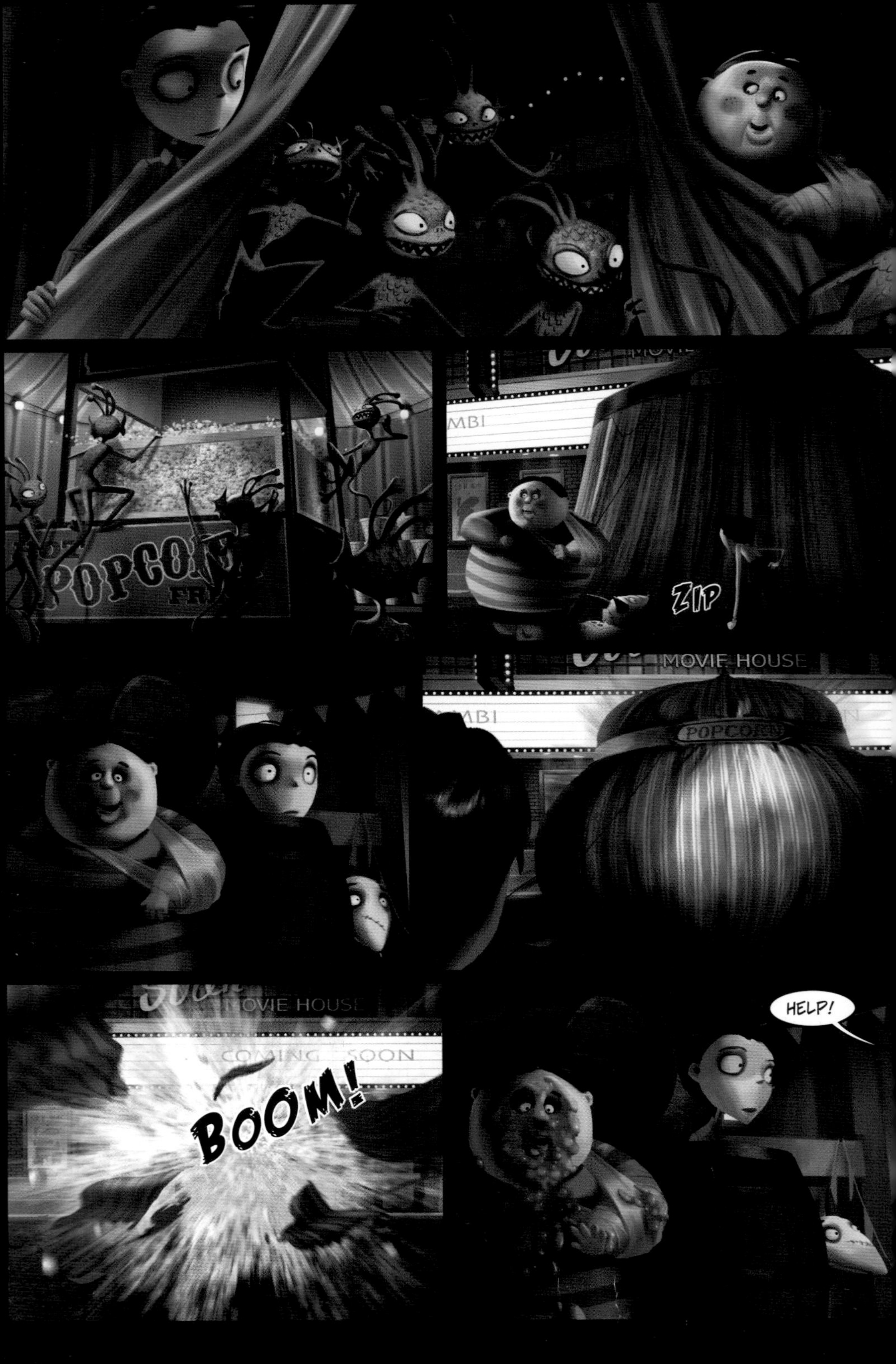
ZIP
MOVIE HOUSE
MOVIE HOUSE
COMING SOON
BOOM!
HELP!

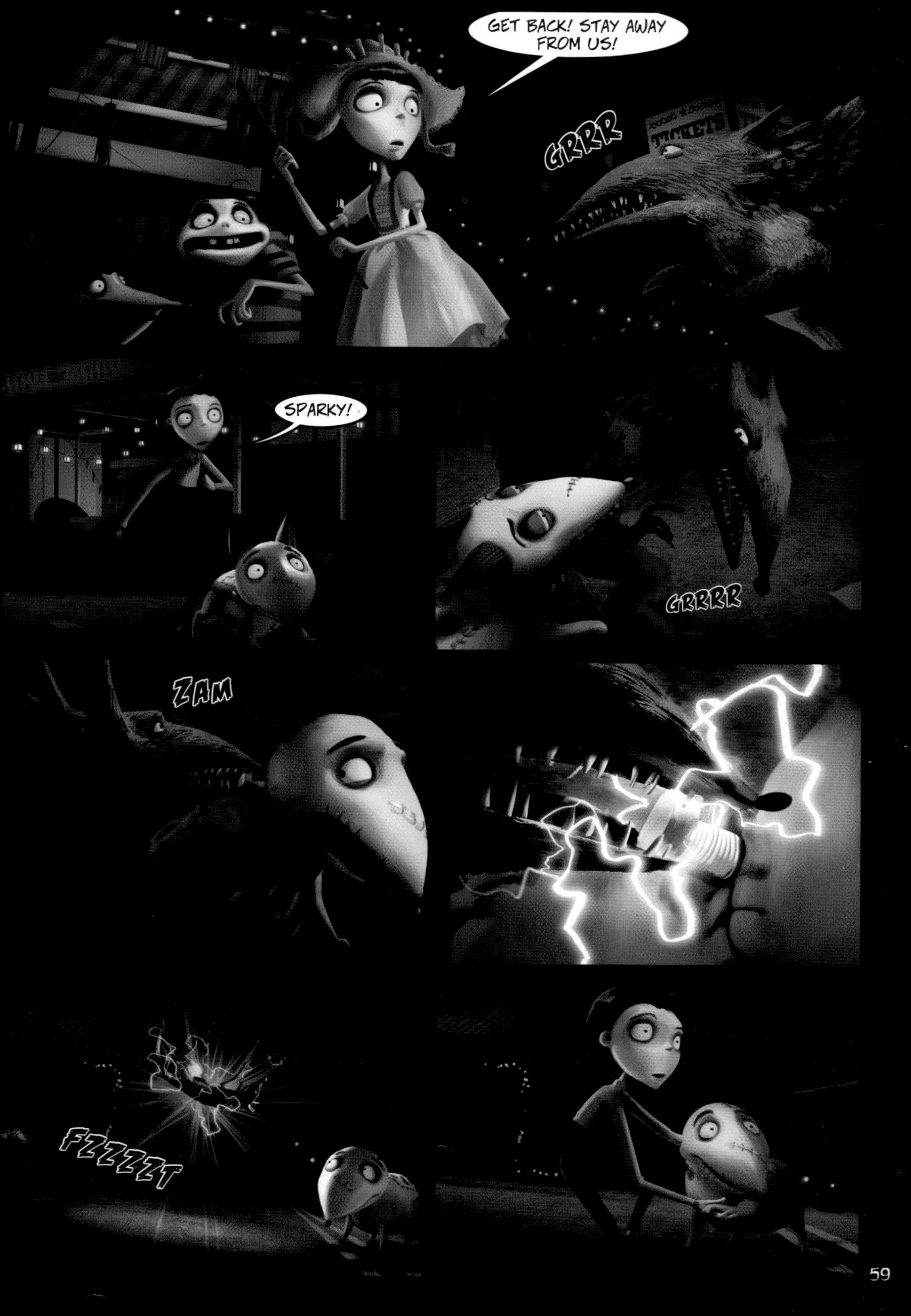
GET BACK! STAY AWAY FROM US!
GRRR
TICKETS
SPARKY!
GRRRR
ZAM
FZZZZT

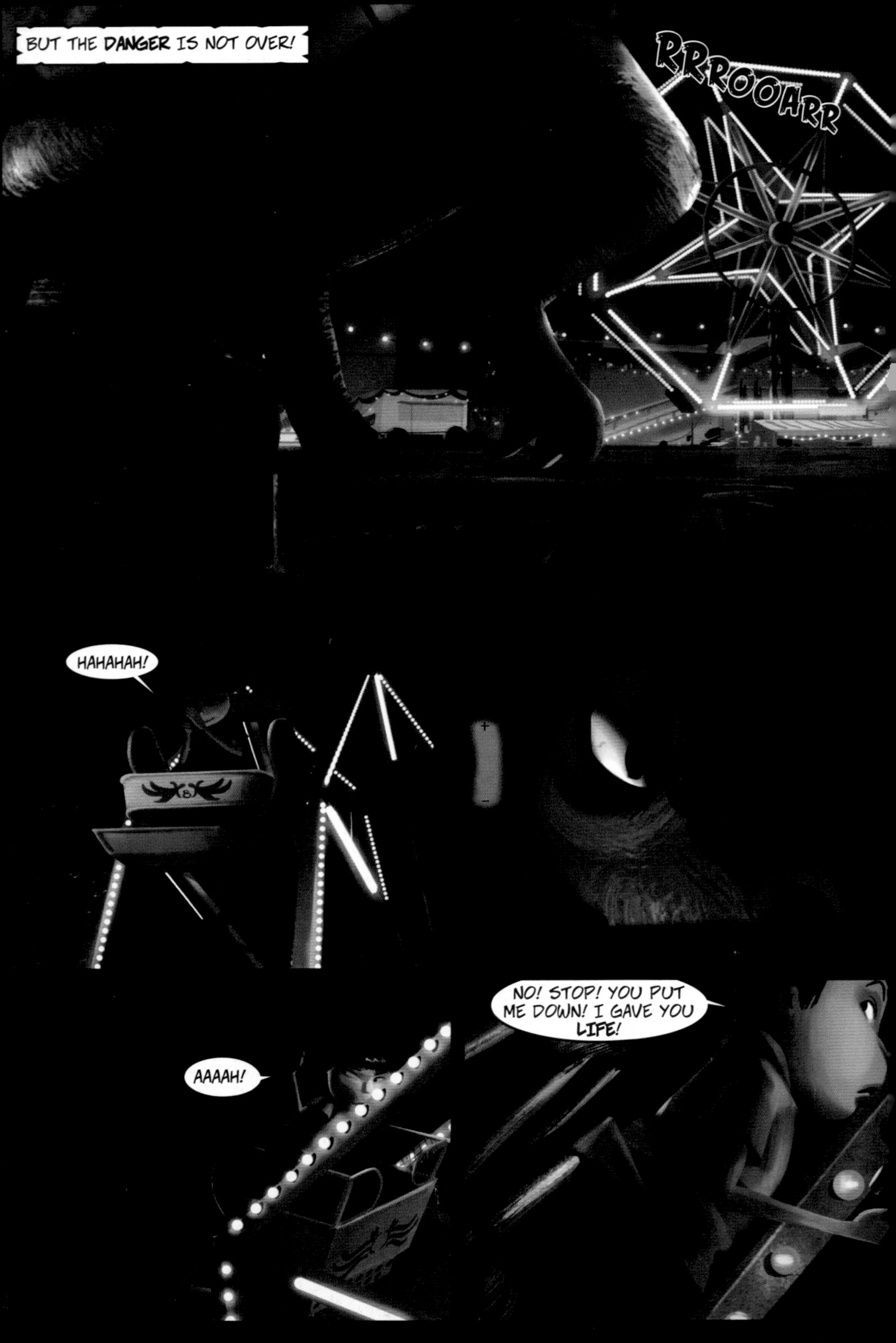
BUT THE DANGER IS NOT OVER!
RRROOARR
HAHAHAH!
NO! STOP! YOU PUT ME DOWN! I GAVE YOU LIFE!
AAAAH!

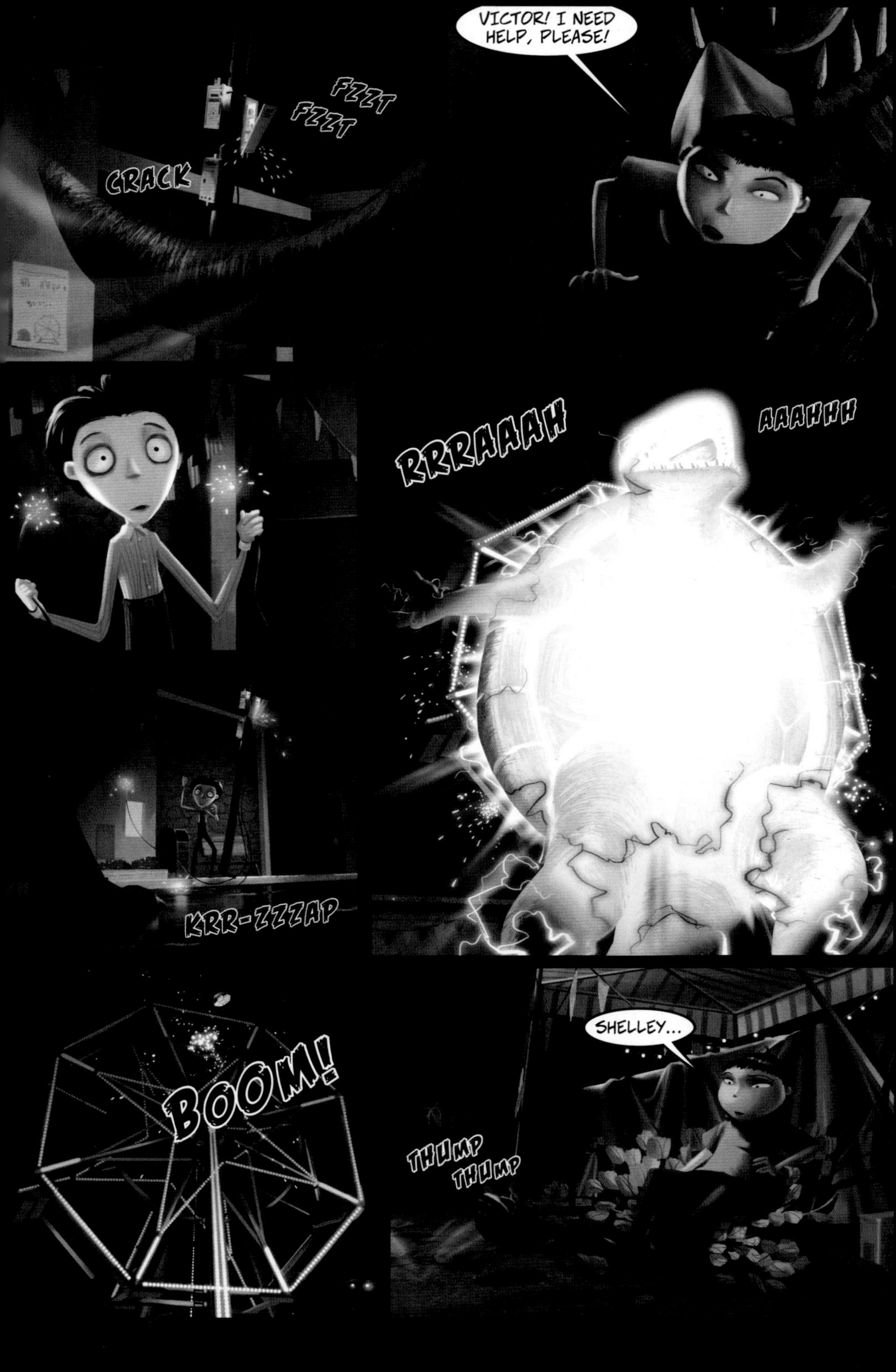

CRACK
FZZT
FZZT
VICTOR! I NEED HELP, PLEASE!
KRR-ZZZAP
RRRAAAH
AAAHHH
BOOM!
THUMP
THUMP
SHELLEY...

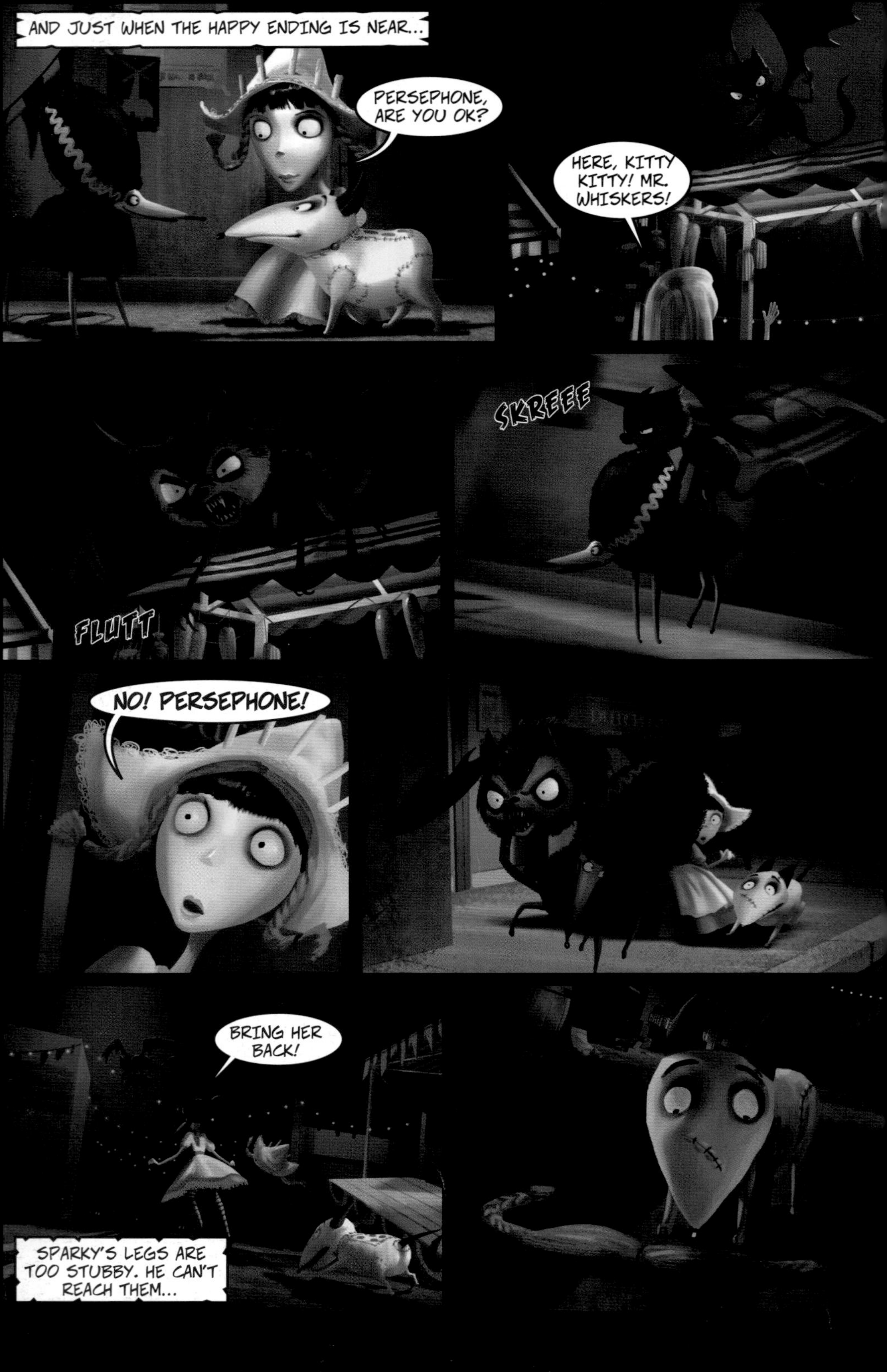
AND JUST WHEN THE HAPPY ENDING IS NEAR...
PERSEPHONE, ARE YOU OK?
HERE, KITTY KITTY! MR. WHISKERS!
FLUTT
SKREEE
NO! PERSEPHONE!
BRING HER BACK!
SPARKY'S LEGS ARE TOO STUBBY. HE CAN'T REACH THEM...

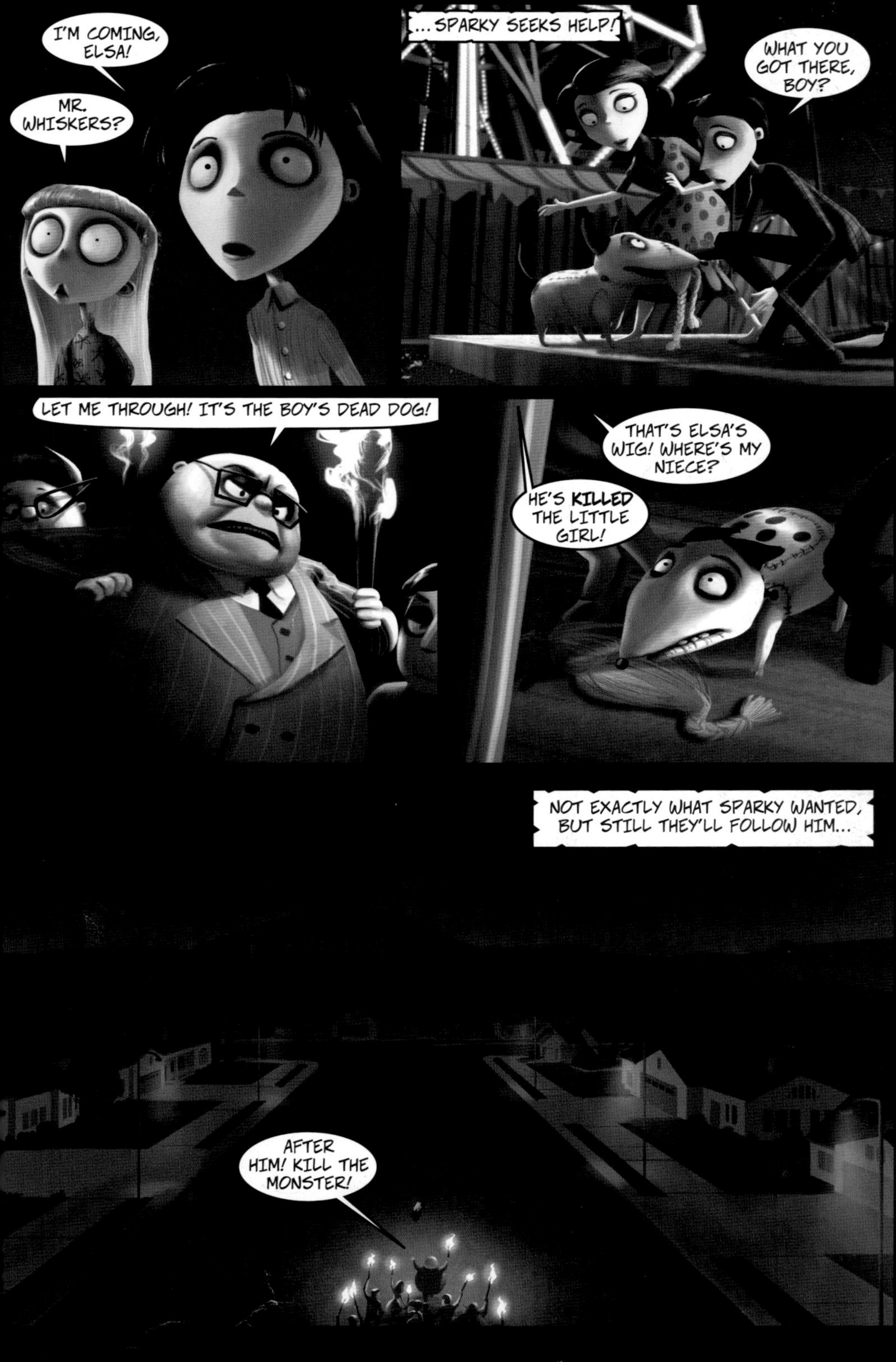
I'M COMING, ELSA!
MR. WHISKERS?
...SPARKY SEEKS HELP!
WHAT YOU GOT THERE, BOY?
LET ME THROUGH! IT'S THE BOY'S DEAD DOG!
THAT'S ELSA'S WIG! WHERE'S MY NIECE?
HE'S KILLED THE LITTLE GIRL!
NOT EXACTLY WHAT SPARKY WANTED, BUT STILL THEY'LL FOLLOW HIM...
AFTER HIM! KILL THE MONSTER!

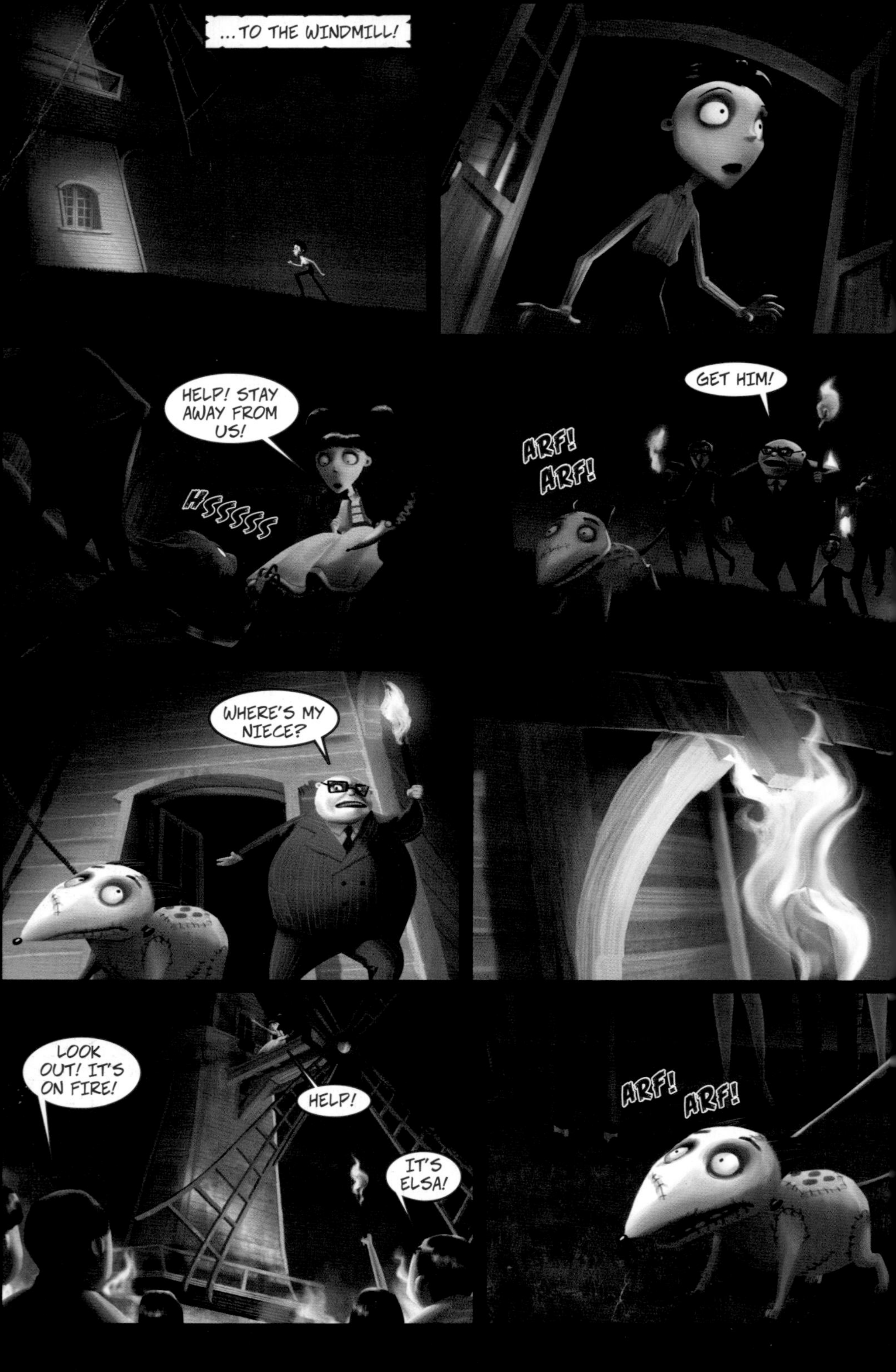
...TO THE WINDMILL!
HELP! STAY AWAY FROM US!
HSSSSS
GET HIM!
ARF! ARF!
WHERE'S MY NIECE?
LOOK OUT! IT'S ON FIRE!
HELP!
IT'S ELSA!
ARF! ARF!

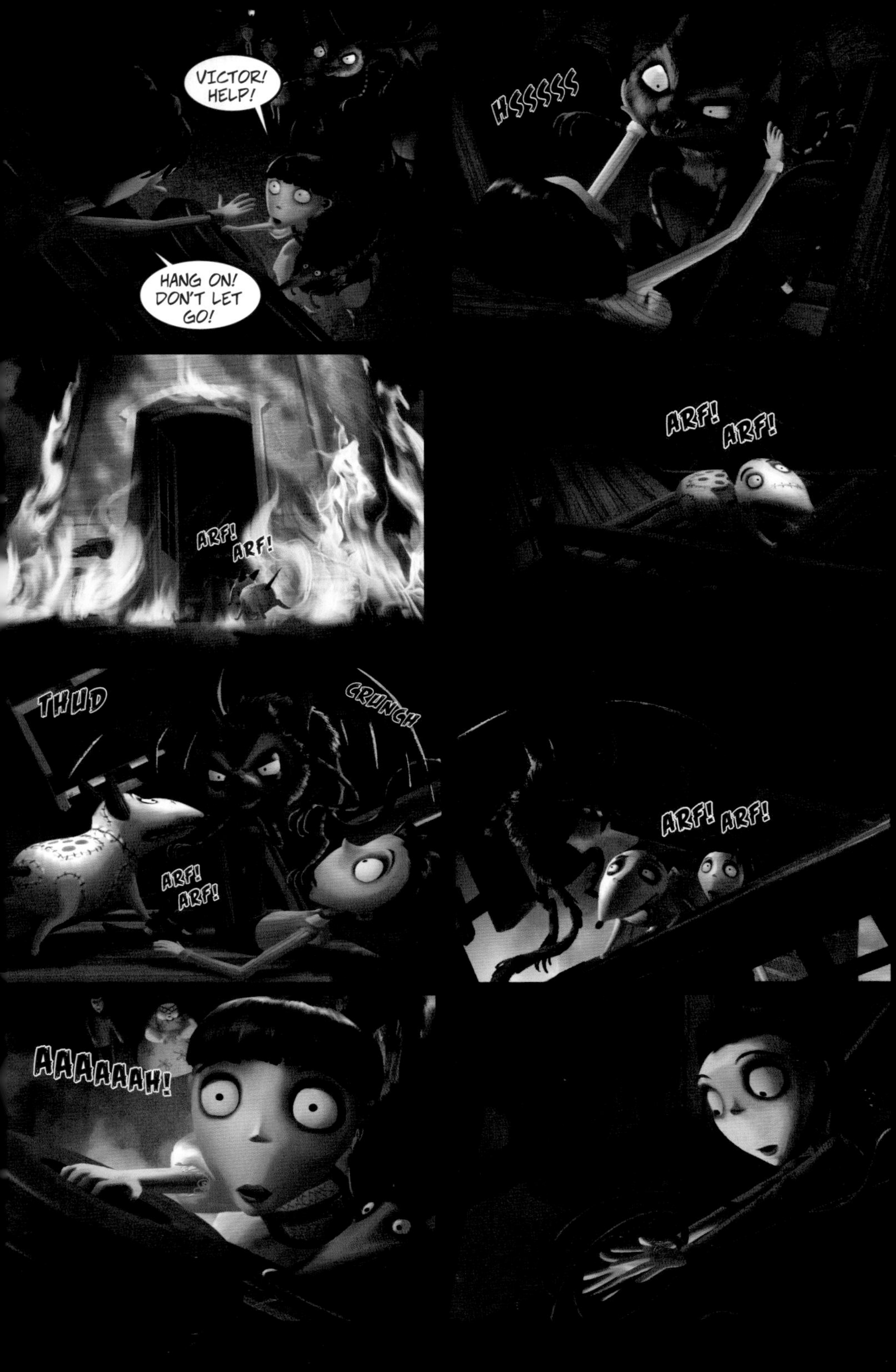
VICTOR! HELP!
HANG ON! DON'T LET GO!
HSSSSSS
ARF! ARF!
ARF! ARF!
THUD
CRUNCH
ARF! ARF!
ARF! ARF!
AAAAAAAH!

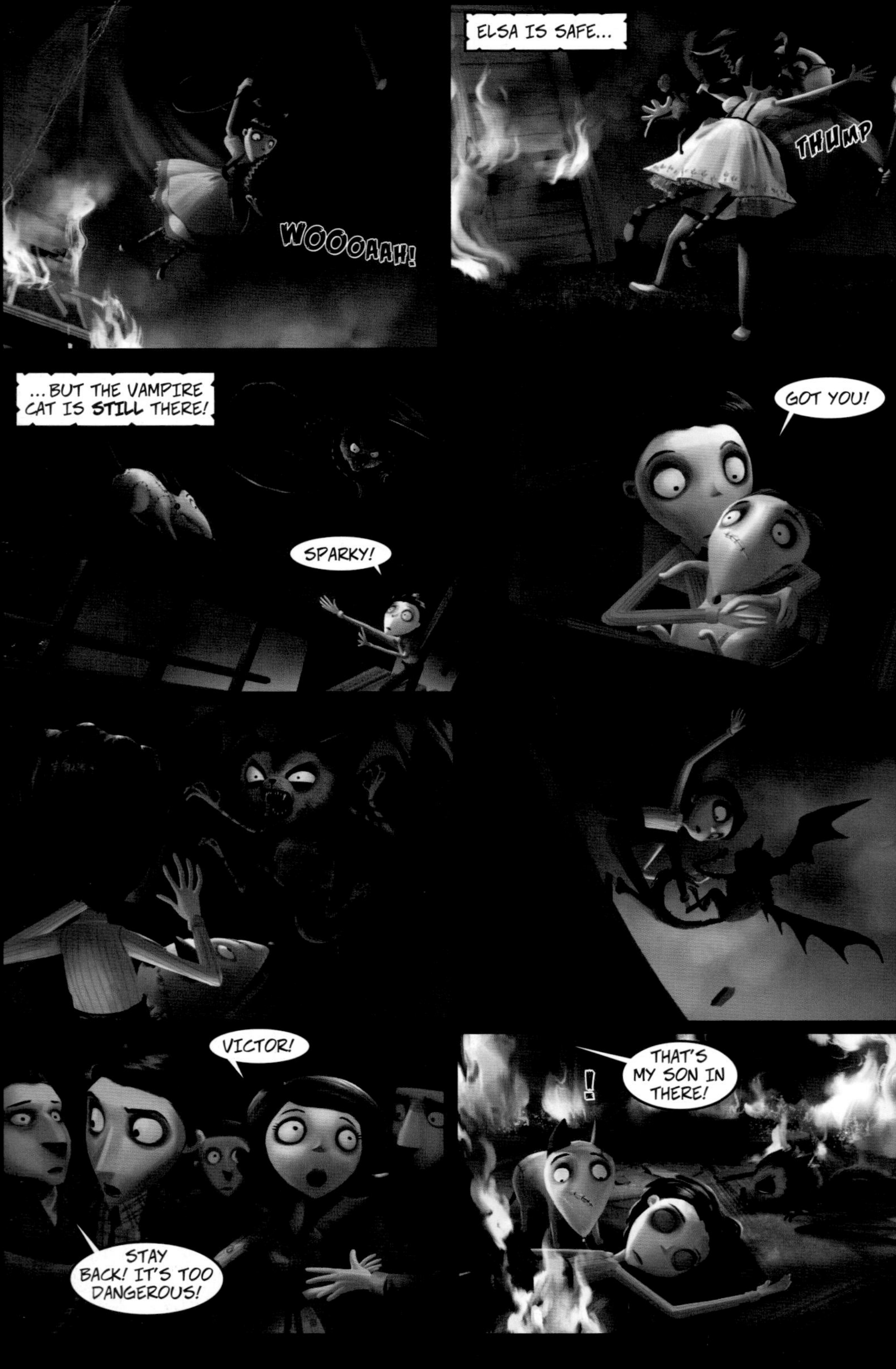
WOOOAAH!
ELSA IS SAFE...
THUMP
...BUT THE VAMPIRE CAT IS STILL THERE!
SPARKY!
GOT YOU!
VICTOR!
STAY BACK! IT'S TOO DANGEROUS!
!
THAT'S MY SON IN THERE!

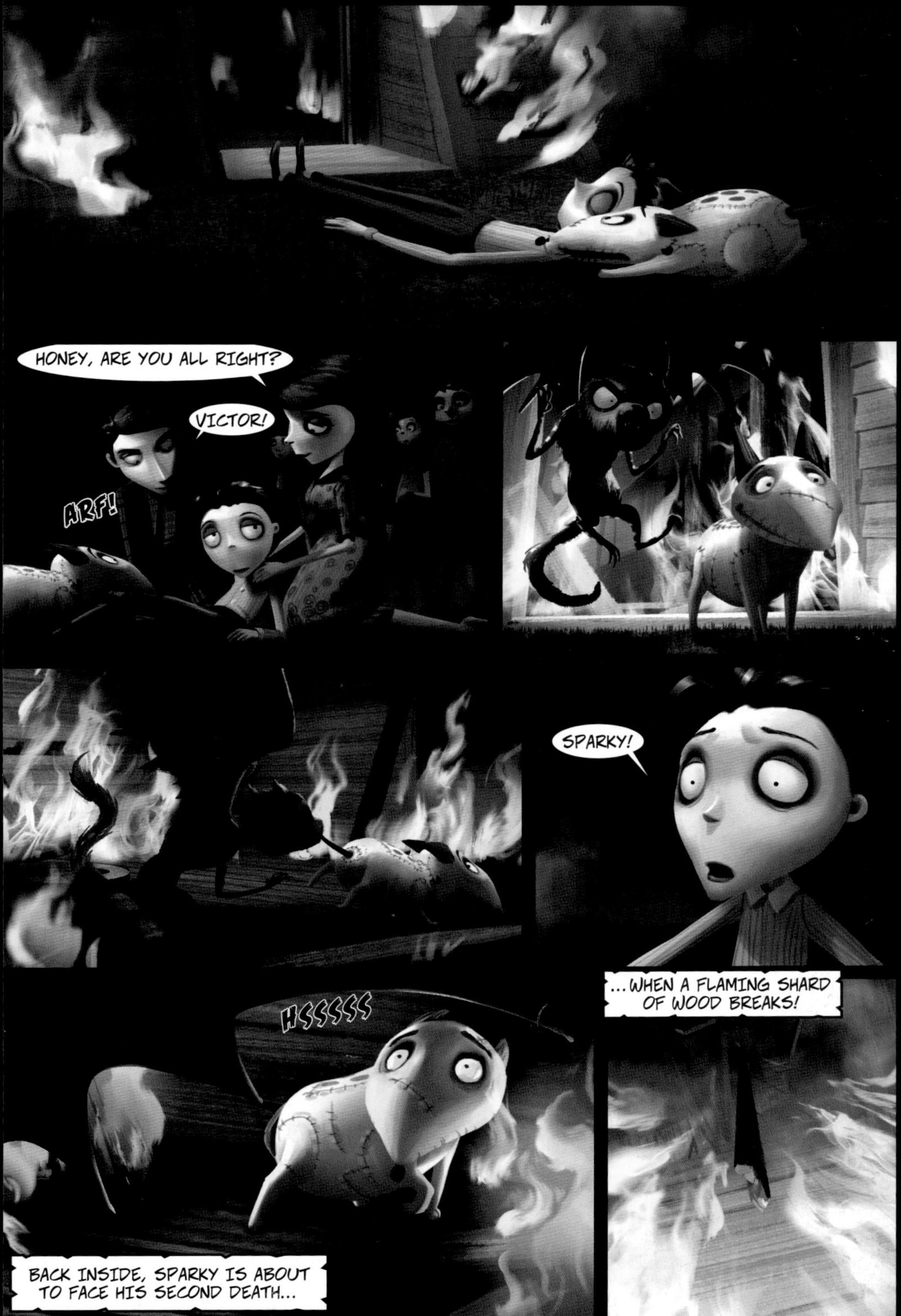
HONEY, ARE YOU ALL RIGHT?
VICTOR!
ARF!
SPARKY!
HSSSSS
BACK INSIDE, SPARKY IS ABOUT TO FACE HIS SECOND DEATH...
...WHEN A FLAMING SHARD OF WOOD BREAKS!

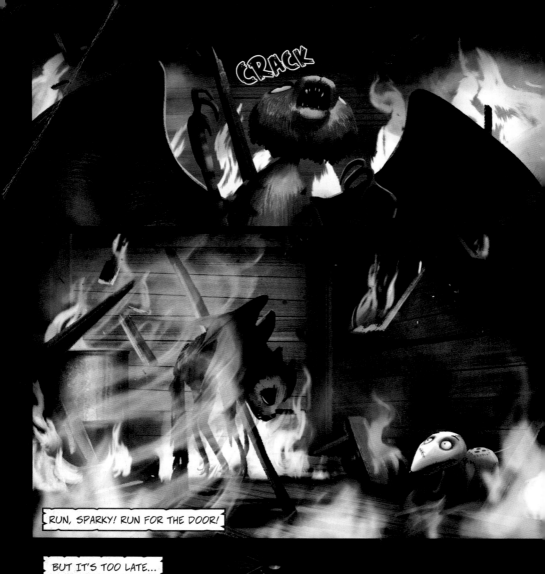

CRACK

RUN, SPARKY! RUN FOR THE DOOR!

BUT IT'S TOO LATE...

KA-BOOM

NOOO! SPARKY!

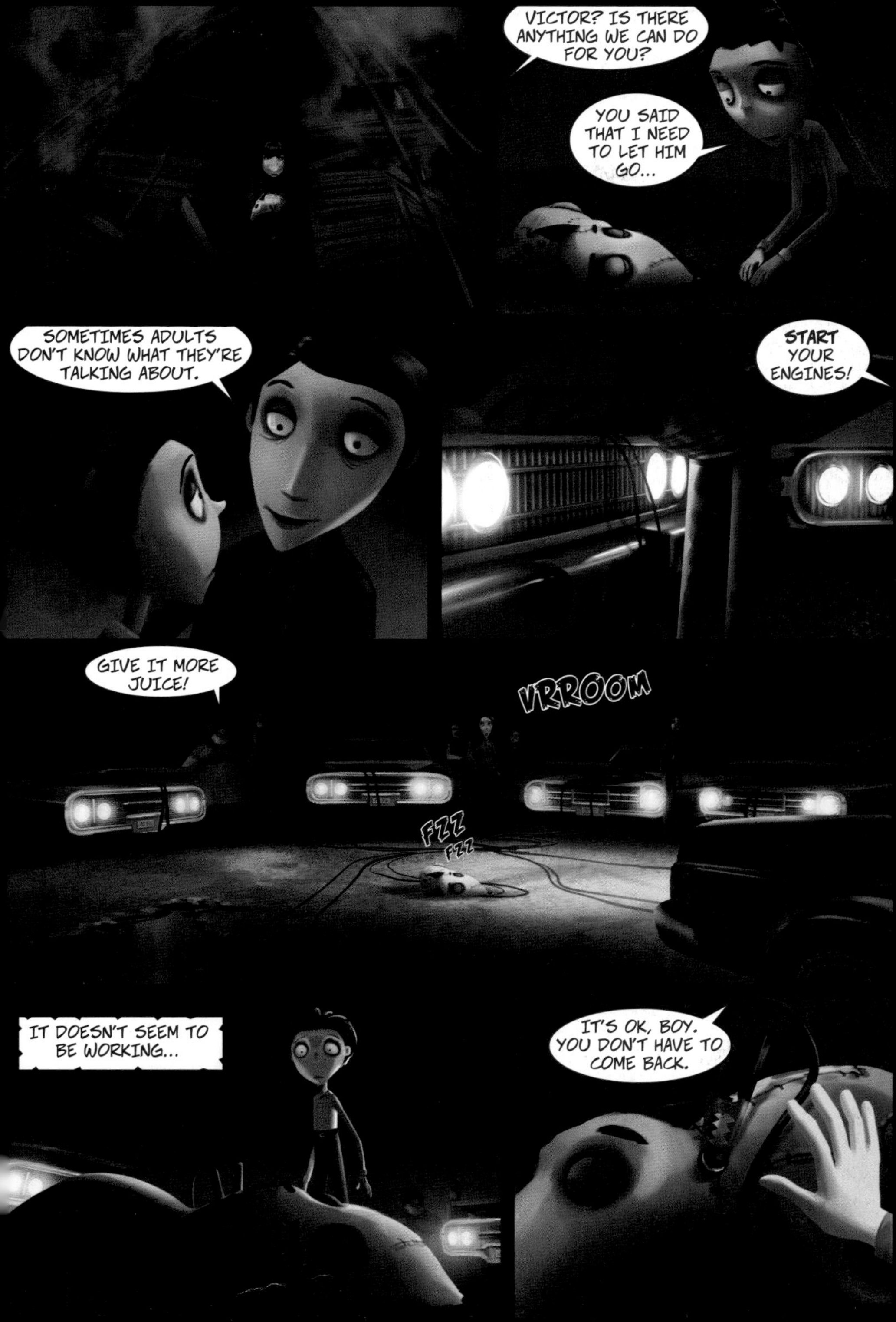
VICTOR? IS THERE ANYTHING WE CAN DO FOR YOU?
YOU SAID THAT I NEED TO LET HIM GO...
SOMETIMES ADULTS DON'T KNOW WHAT THEY'RE TALKING ABOUT.
START YOUR ENGINES!
GIVE IT MORE JUICE!
VRROOM
FZZ FZZ
IT DOESN'T SEEM TO BE WORKING...
IT'S OK, BOY. YOU DON'T HAVE TO COME BACK.

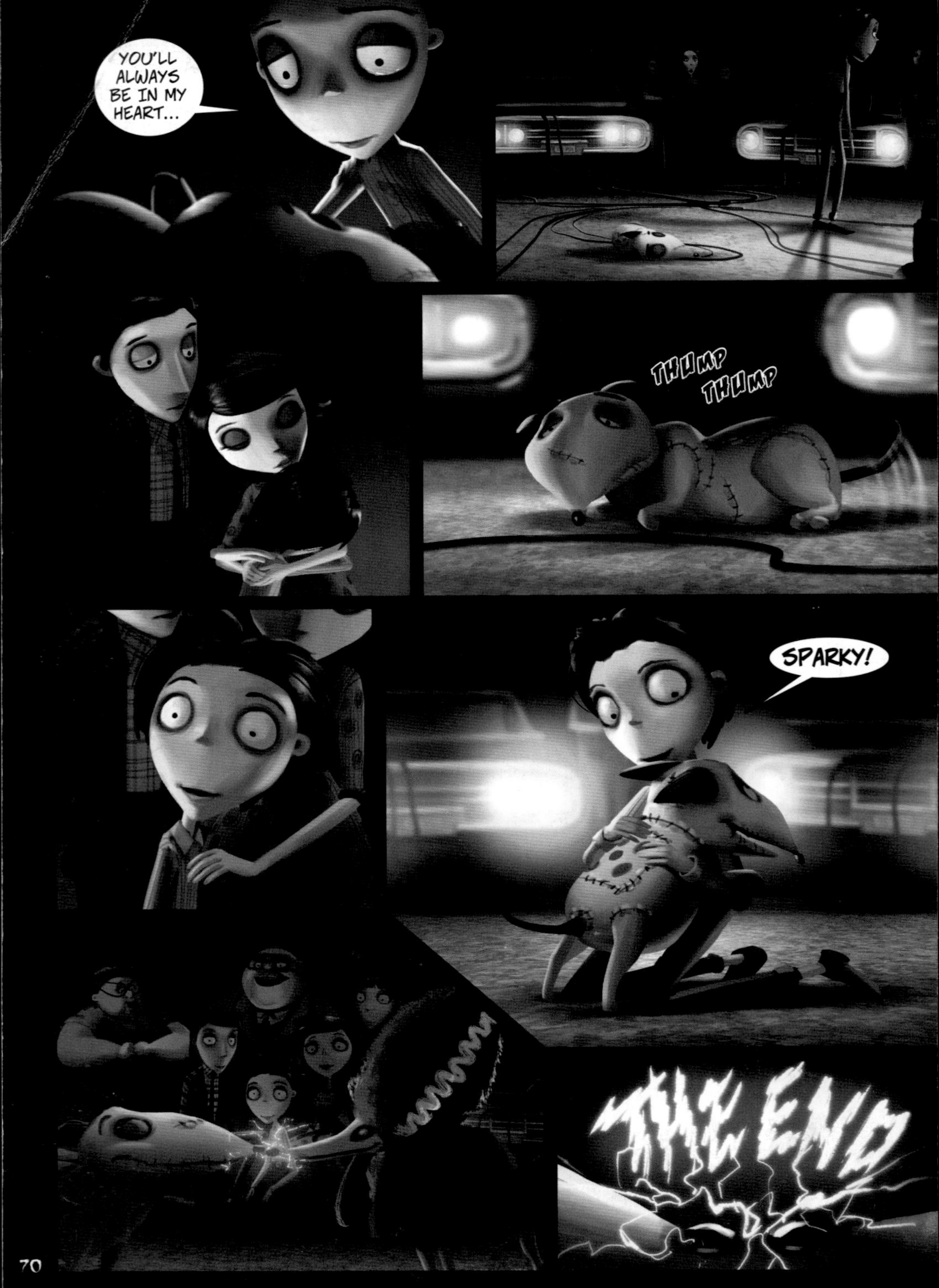
YOU'LL ALWAYS BE IN MY HEART...
THUMP THUMP
SPARKY!
THE END

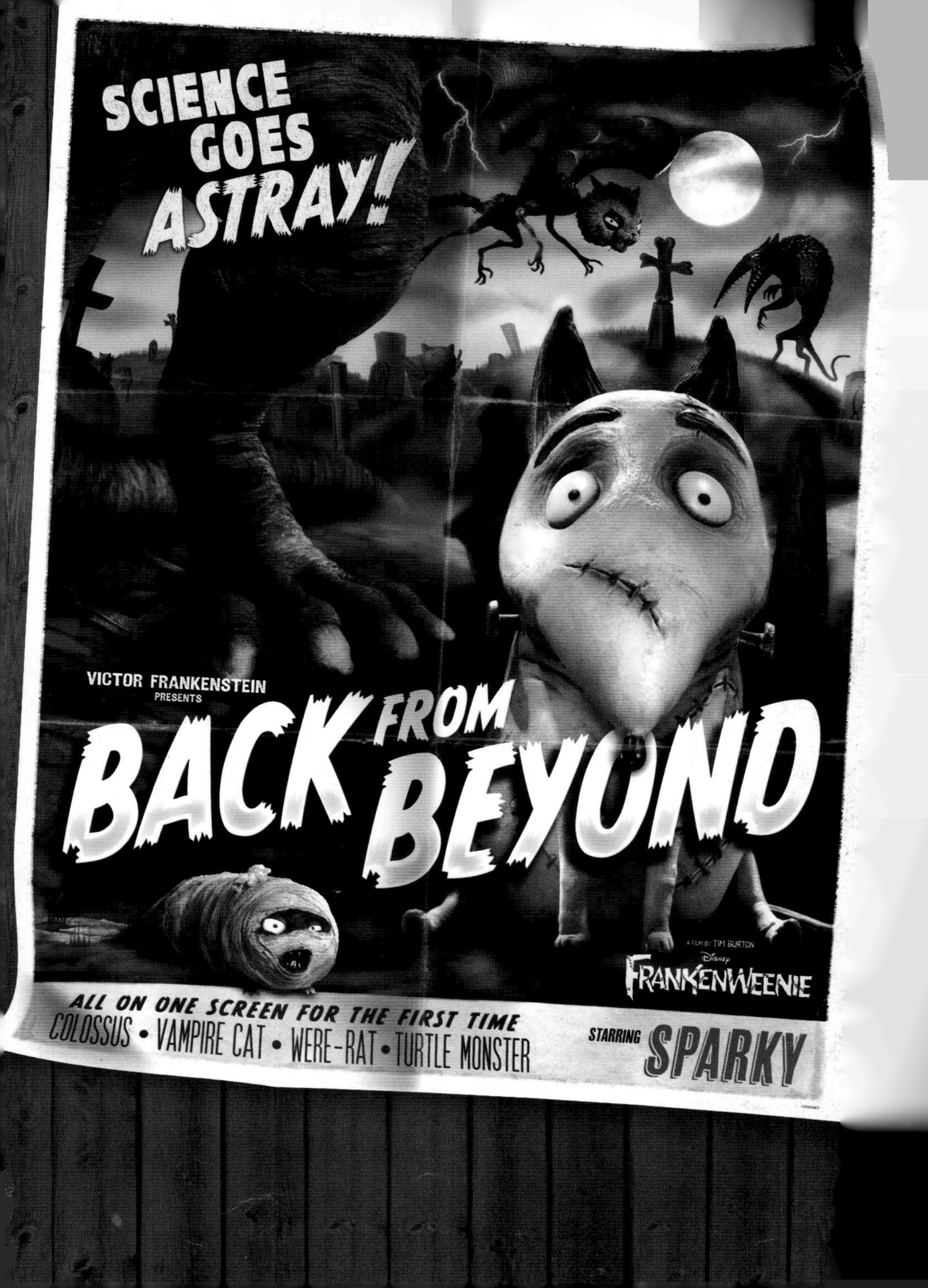
SCIENCE GOES ASTRAY!
VICTOR FRANKENSTEIN PRESENTS
BACK FROM BEYOND
A FILM BY TIM BURTON
DISNEY
FRANKENWEENIE
ALL ON ONE SCREEN FOR THE FIRST TIME
COLOSSUS • VAMPIRE CAT • WERE-RAT • TURTLE MONSTER
STARRING SPARKY

Published by Disney Press, an imprint of Disney Book Group.

For information address Disney Press, 1101 Flower Street, Glendale, California, 91201.
Printed in the United States of America

First Edition

ISBN 978-1-4231-7658-9

SUSTAINABLE FORESTRY INITIATIVE
Certified Chain of Custody
At Least 20% Certified Forest Cont
www.sfiprogram.org
SFI-00993
For Text Only